Welcome to the S̶ ̶ ̶ ̶ ̶!

Did you ever get so ca̶ ̶ ̶ ̶ ̶ ̶ ̶ ̶ ̶ ̶y or something that yo̶ ̶ ̶ ̶ ̶ ̶ ̶ ̶ ̶ ̶e doing it in the first p̶ ̶ ̶ ̶ ̶ ̶ ̶ ̶ away. It happens to all of us. But it always seems like when I get swept up in the excitement, the chemical plant is right there . . . waiting to take me away. Let me explain:

I'm Alex Mack. I was just another average kid until my first day of junior high.

One minute I'm walking home from school—the next there's a *crash!* A truck from the Paradise Valley Chemical plant overturns in front of me, and I'm drenched in some weird chemical.

And since then—well, nothing's been the same. I can move objects with my mind, shoot electrical charges through my fingertips, and morph into a liquid shape . . . which is handy when I get in a tight spot!

My best friend, Ray, thinks it's cool—and my sister Annie thinks I'm a science project.

They're the only two people who know about my new powers. I can't let anyone else find out—not even my parents—because I know the chemical plant wants to find me and turn me into some experiment.

But you know something? I guess I'm not so average anymore!

The Secret World of Alex Mack™

Alex, You're Glowing!
Bet You Can't!
Bad News Babysitting!
Witch Hunt!
Mistaken Identity!
Cleanup Catastrophe!

Available from MINSTREL Books

the secret world of

ALEX MACK ™

Cleanup Catastrophe!

Cathy East Dubowski

A
MINSTREL® BOOK

Published by POCKET BOOKS
New York   London   Toronto   Sydney   Tokyo   Singapore

This book is a work of fiction. Names, characters, places and incidents are products of the author's imagination or are used fictitiously. Any resemblance to actual events or locales or persons, living or dead, is entirely coincidental.

A MINSTREL PAPERBACK *Original*

 A Minstrel Book published by
POCKET BOOKS, a division of Simon & Schuster Inc.
1230 Avenue of the Americas, New York, NY 10020

ISBN: 0-671-56308-4

First Minstrel Books printing April 1996

10 9 8 7 6 5 4 3 2 1

Cover photography by Blake Little

Printed in the U.S.A.

To Lauren—
Thanks for watching *The Secret World of Alex Mack* with me.
Now clean up your room! (I'll help!)
Love, Mom

CHAPTER 1

"Alex, don't you know there's a fine for littering?"

Sprawled out on her bed, Alex Mack lowered her magazine and made a face at her older sister. "Very funny, Annie. Maybe if you ever get tired of being a brilliant scientist, you can become a stand-up comedian."

"Really, Alex!" Annie stared at the middle of the floor as if she'd spotted a cockroach. With forefinger and thumb, she picked up one of Alex's purple-striped socks. It was definitely ready for the laundry.

"Ugh!" Annie dropped the sock onto a pile of clothes half shoved under Alex's bed. "It's reached toxic proportions in here, Alex. This room should be evacuated before someone is contaminated."

"There's the door," Alex said, jerking her thumb toward the doorway. "What's stopping you?"

The two sisters glared at each other across the invisible line that divided their room.

And then they burst out laughing.

"Well, it's true, Alex," Annie said with a grin as she sat down at her desk. "Come on, admit it. Your side of the room should be declared a hazard to humans."

Alex surveyed the room she'd shared with her sister since the day she was born. When they were little, the two sides of the room had looked like mirror images of each other. Twin beds with matching pink bedspreads. Identical stuffed animals from their grandparents lined up neatly on each bed. Though there were two years between them, Alex and Annie had been so much alike. Sometimes their mom had even dressed them in matching outfits, especially on holidays.

Alex had loved that when she was little. She'd loved being exactly like her big sister, whom she adored.

Now? Well, fourteen-year-old Alex still loved her sister. But somehow, somewhere, when she wasn't looking, everything had changed. She and Annie weren't anything alike anymore. Far from it. It was as if they came from two different planets.

Take their room, for example. It definitely had a split personality.

Annie's side was neat and organized. Dozens of framed awards lined the wall next to a poster of the solar system and another of Albert Einstein. Her bed was made up as neatly as a bed in a department store ad, and her clothes were hung up in the closet or folded away in her dresser. Annie's desk looked as if it belonged to a college professor, with thick science books arranged alphabetically next to neat stacks of paper and notebooks. Even Annie's handwriting was neat and elegant.

Then there was Alex's side of the room. Her side had more of a lived-in look. Her walls were plastered with posters of rock stars and cute animals and pictures cut out of magazines. Her humongous collection of crazy hats cluttered a hat rack above the door. Her bed was only half made, books were scattered everywhere, and clothes were draped over the furniture.

And her desk? It was so piled up with junk that it was hard to tell it was a desk. Alex usually did her homework curled up on her bed. But she kind of liked it that way—it was cosier.

It wouldn't look all that messy, Alex thought, *if I had a room to myself. Or if I had a normal sister.*

Annie's neat side just made Alex's side look messier. Comparing herself to Annie always made Alex feel kind of bummed out. Kind of ordinary. Kind of boring.

And that was the story of her life.

Everything about Annie was perfect. She was so smart that all her teachers adored her. She'd probably win a Nobel Prize for Science one day, they all said. Even her parents said it.

On TV and in the movies, smart kids were always dorks. But not Annie. Annie was pretty, with dark shoulder-length hair and big brown eyes. Worst of all, she always seemed so sure of herself, as if she knew exactly what she was doing.

Sometimes Alex didn't know what she was doing or how to do it. Sometimes she felt as if she didn't have a clue. *I'm just . . . just plain ordinary me. Ordinary looks. An ordinary personality. Talents? Hmm . . . Can't think of a single one.*

Alex could usually pull a string of B's at school, but A's? For Alex trying for A's felt like chasing butterflies without a net.

Being Annie Mack's little sister meant that she could never do anything really great—'cause Annie would always be greater. How could Alex possibly compete with a sister who scored 100 on the perfection meter every time?

"Hey, Alex!" Annie teased. "Are you turning this into a landfill area for the entire town, or do you plan on cleaning up anytime before the millennium?"

"Okay, okay!" Alex said. She hated it when her sister used big words, but she knew Annie couldn't help herself. "I promise I'll clean up a little." She scooped up a pile of dirty clothes and carried them to the closet. Then she dumped them on the closet floor, closed the door, and brushed off her hands. "Ta-da! How's that?"

Annie rolled her eyes and tried hard not to laugh. "Give me a break, Alex!"

"Okay, then," Alex said with a mischievous grin. "How about this?"

She scrunched her face and squinted her eyes, concentrating hard as she stared at several books scattered on her desk, some of them still open.

Suddenly the books snapped shut, rose into the air, and stacked themselves into a neat floating pile.

Next Alex glared at the jean jacket draped across her desk chair. Sleeves flapping, it flew to the hook on the back of the door.

Concentrate! Alex told herself.

Soon books, pens, stuffed animals, and underwear floated in the air, whirling like planets in a tiny solar system.

"Alex!" Annie scolded her sister. "What if Mom and Dad see?" But in spite of herself, Annie stared in wonder at the magic happening before her eyes.

Alex grinned. Yes, she was ordinary all right. Except for one teeny tiny little thing.

On the first day of junior high school she'd been accidentally drenched in an experimental chemical called GC 161, produced at the Paradise Valley Chemical plant. Besides being really gross and gunky, GC 161 was toxic, and it had given Alex some pretty outrageous powers. Now she could float things, zap things, and morph into a weird silvery Jell-O kind of puddle and ooze down drainpipes and under doors.

Her new powers should have changed Alex's life in a majorly cool way. But she still had to show up for junior high school every day. And she still had to do homework every night. And even though she had these incredible powers, Annie was still smarter than she was.

The worst part? Annie had made her promise not to tell anyone about her magical abilities. Not even her mom or dad knew. Annie was afraid that if her sister's secret came out, the scientists at Paradise Valley Chemical would turn Alex into a human guinea pig and perform all kinds of weird experiments on her. She also feared that the government might shut down the company. Then her dad and almost everybody else in town would be out of a job. They couldn't let that happen!

At least Annie paid a lot more attention to Alex

these days. But Annie would probably win some kind of international science award one day for the experiments she was doing on her mutated sister.

"Annie! Alex!" their dad called to them from the bottom of the stairs. "Supper's almost ready. Would you please come down and set the table?"

Startled by her father's voice, Alex lost her concentration and the airborne books, clothes, and junk clunked to the floor.

Annie jumped up and streaked over to slam and lock the door in case their parents came up.

At that moment a black teddy bear with a red bow tie crashed onto Annie's desk, knocking over her half-filled glass of ice water. "Alex!" Annie screeched. She snatched at her papers as water sloshed across her desk.

Alex ran out and grabbed a towel from the bathroom and flung it onto the desk, trying to soak up the spill.

Glaring at Alex, Annie snatched the towel and managed to mop up the water before it reached her books. Then she tossed the soggy towel back at her sister. "Alex! You almost ruined my report. And it's due tomorrow!" Annie shook her head as she examined her papers for damage. "You can't imagine how many hours it took me to print out these charts on the color printer at school. Oooh! I wish I had my own room!"

"I'm sorry, Annie," Alex said. "Really! I—"

"Annie! Alex!" they heard their mom shouting up the stairs. "Supper—now!"

Annie opened the door and poked her head out. "Coming, Mom!" Then she turned back to Alex with an exasperated look on her face. "Alex, how many times do I have to tell you? You've got to be more responsible about using your powers! What if Dad or Mom had walked in while you were floating things around the room?"

Alex plopped down on her bed and stared at the scuffed toes of her brown leather hiking boots. The playful good mood in the room had evaporated like the fizz in a can of flat soda. "Sorry, Annie," she mumbled. "I was just trying to clean up."

Annie sighed and sat down on the edge of the bed. She laid her hand on her sister's shoulder. "Look, Alex. I'm sorry I sounded so mean. But I don't want anything bad to happen to you, okay? If the people at the plant find out about you, you could spend the rest of your life as a lab rat inside Paradise Valley Chemical's research and development department. Who knows what kind of experiments they'd put you through? And they wouldn't be as careful with you as I am, because they'd only care about the results of their experiment—not about you or your feelings."

"I know, I know," Alex said.

"Believe me," Annie teased, "it would be even worse than eighth grade at Danielle Atron Junior High School!"

Alex laughed. "That bad, huh?"

"Just be more careful, okay?" Annie smiled. "Come on, let's go set the table. I'm starved."

Alex dragged herself off the bed and headed for the door. *My life is the pits*, she thought with a sigh.

The only thing special about her entire ordinary existence was something she had to keep a secret. So she was still stuck living in Annie's shadow. Still stuck wandering through junior high school without a compass or even a good-luck charm. "Welcome to the secret world of Alex Mack," she muttered. "Just don't tell anybody anything about it."

Alex jumped backward as Annie suddenly rushed back into the room, shouting, "I almost forgot!" Grinning, she plucked a letter from the notebook on her desk and waved it in the air as if it held a winning lottery ticket. "I got some great news in the mail today. I've been saving it for dinner. Hurry, Alex!" Then she flew out of the room.

Alex followed her sister down the stairs. Annie propped her letter on the table between the salt and pepper shakers. Then she hummed happily as she and Alex set the dining room table.

Their mom and dad carried in several steaming dishes, and then they all sat down to eat.

"Mmmm," George Mack murmured as he breathed in deeply. "Honey, I love your turkey meat loaf."

Barbara smiled. "Thanks, dear. Well, everybody, dig in."

Annie couldn't wait. She reached for her letter. "Mom, Dad, I've got some good news to share." She cleared her throat as she pulled a crisp sheet of stationery from the envelope and unfolded it.

Alex propped her head in her hand and dug little canals in her mashed potatoes with her fork. What was it this time? Another science award? A commendation from the president? An invitation to tea from the queen of England?

"Remember the paper I wrote about my midterm chemistry project?" Annie asked. "Well, I didn't tell anyone, but I submitted it to my favorite magazine. And guess what? They're going to publish it!"

"Oh, Annie, that's wonderful!" Barbara Mack exclaimed. "Why didn't you tell us before?"

"I wanted to surprise you!" Annie gushed. "The acceptance letter just came today. Isn't it exciting, Dad?"

"Yes, Annie," George Mack said. "This is very impressive."

"Here—let me read you part of the letter," Annie said.

" 'And we might add,' " Annie read aloud, " 'that

you are the youngest author ever to have a paper published in *Scientific Endeavors Quarterly Journal.' "*

So that was it, Alex thought. Some boring paper Annie had written was going to be published in some dumb magazine that nobody but other science brains ever read. And most of them were probably at least three or four times older than Annie.

"That's quite an honor," Mr. Mack said. "I'm very proud of you, Annie."

Annie beamed, and Alex slumped down in her chair, feeling awful. For some reason, getting published in this magazine from boresville was important to Annie. Alex knew she should have been glad for Annie, but instead she was acting like a bratty little sister who couldn't share her big sister's happiness.

Alex couldn't help wondering: Would her mom and dad ever sound that excited about something *she* did?

CHAPTER 2

The next morning a white stretch limo zoomed around the curving road that led into Paradise Valley.

In the backseat a dark-haired, well-dressed executive barked orders into a cellular phone as she flipped through her leather appointment book. Danielle Atron was chief executive officer of Paradise Valley Chemical. Her driver had just picked her up at the airport after a four-day business trip. She was glad to be home, eager to get back to the office.

Suddenly she yelled to the chaffeur, "Driver! Slow down. Now."

The driver obeyed, tapping the brakes. The limo slowed to a crawl as it passed a large brick and marble sign. Surrounded by well-tended flowers and shrubbery, the sign read, WELCOME TO PARADISE VALLEY, HOME OF PARADISE VALLEY CHEMICAL COMPANY.

Danielle smiled as she gazed at the sign. This whole town had been built with Paradise Valley Chemical money. Nearly everyone in town worked for or earned a living from the plant.

And Danielle ran the company. Why, they'd even named the junior high school after her.

Danielle smiled smugly. This was *her* town.

"Drive on!" she called to the driver. He pressed the accelerator, and Danielle opened her briefcase to look over some files.

A few minutes later—

Bang!

The limo jerked, and Danielle's papers slipped to the floor.

Thud-thud-thud-thud-thud.

The limo swerved onto the side of the road, kicking up gravel and a huge cloud of dust. Danielle's seat belt crushed wrinkles into her linen suit as the car jolted to a stop.

"I don't have time in my schedule for this!" Danielle shouted at the driver. "What happened?"

"I think it's a blowout, Ms. Atron," he answered politely. "I'll—"

"Well, fix it—quick, whatever it is."

"Yes, Ms. Atron."

As her driver scrambled out, Danielle crossed her legs and jabbed the buttons on her cellular phone.

She tapped her polished red nails impatiently on the armrest as she listened to the phone ring.

"Paradise Valley Chemical," her secretary answered. "How may I help—?"

"It's me! I'm in the limo," Danielle interrupted. "We've had some kind of stupid blowout or something. You'll have to rearrange my schedule."

A few moments later she hung up and pulled out a bottle of chilled mineral water from the limo's small refrigerator. She wrenched off the top, popped in a straw, then stepped out of the car so the driver could change the tire.

"Ewww!" Danielle stared down in disgust at one of her black patent-leather pumps. She'd stepped into some squishy roadside litter. Stuck to the bottom of her shoe was a burger wrapper, with a smelly chunk of half-chewed cheeseburger still in it. A few squashed fries were on the ground nearby.

A fly landed on the pointed toe of her shoe.

"Disgusting!" Fuming, Danielle marched over to a patch of grass to wipe the cheese and ketchup off her shoe.

Then she glared across the broad field with her fists planted on her hips. Aluminum cans, broken amber bottles, and scraps of paper poked up through the weeds. Buzzing insects dive-bombed some murky water pooled in an old tire. A sun-faded T-shirt was mashed into the mud.

"People are such pigs," she said to no one in particular. "How dare they!" This was her town. And this trashy roadside was a stain on her image. She liked things neat. Orderly. Clean and sanitized. In other words, perfect. Litter did not make her look good.

Danielle stalked over to the car—careful to step around the rotting leftovers—and grabbed her phone. She punched in more numbers and waited, dabbing at her perspiring forehead with a monogrammed linen handkerchief.

"Barbara Mack speaking."

Danielle paid Alex's mother's public relations firm a huge fee each month to make Paradise Valley Chemical look good. It was important to Danielle that she and the company have a sparkling reputation. Now more than ever it was urgent that none of their work be questioned. Their genetic research on the chemical GC 161 was top secret . . . and not exactly legal. But the company was on the verge of an astounding breakthrough that would make everyone forget that they had bent a few rules and regulations. Danielle was sure of it. Some day very soon GC 161 would earn Paradise Valley Chemical a fortune, and Danielle Atron would be famous.

"Barbara, darling," Danielle ordered into the phone. "Drop whatever it is you're doing. I've got an urgent project for you."

CHAPTER 3

Alex jammed her algebra book into her stuffed locker, clicked the combination lock shut, and spun the dial. Then she turned and squinted suspiciously at her best friend, Ray Alvarado. "Say that again?"

"I said I love assemblies," Ray repeated with a dimpled grin.

"Really?"

"Yeah," he said brightly. "Especially when they get me out of math class."

Alex laughed and high-fived him as they moved into the rowdy river of kids flowing toward the school auditorium.

"Hey, Alex," Ray whispered with a grin. "Too bad you can't use your powers to change the clocks every day so I never have to go to math."

Alex grinned. She knew Ray was kidding. He was the only person besides Annie who knew about Alex's unusual powers, and he understood how important it was to keep quiet about them. She and Ray had been next-door neighbors and best friends since they were babies, and Alex trusted him completely with her secret. Besides, he wouldn't dare squeal on her. She knew too many of his secrets!

The only problem was that Ray thought her powers were the coolest thing that had ever happened. He was always dreaming up outrageous ways to use her powers for fun and profit.

"How about levitating Joe Burns to Mars so I can sit next to Alicia Pienkowski during assembly?" he joked.

"Ray! Shhh!" she whispered, giggling.

"Why not? I'd do it for you!" he whispered back.

As they turned a corner, two of Alex's other best friends, Nicole Wilson and Robyn Russo, rushed out of civics class.

"Hey, guys, do you know what's going on?" Nicole asked Alex and Ray.

"We haven't got a clue," Ray said.

"I was supposed to do an oral report this morning," Nicole went on. "It's about how the current government is destroying our First Amendment rights as students. I was really psyched."

Nicole was one of the only kids Alex knew who

actually liked to give oral reports. Of course, Nicole believed her mission in life was to educate the ignorant masses about whatever she was totally into at the moment—and it changed almost daily.

Nicole shrugged. "But who knows, maybe we're in for some good news."

Robyn sighed. "I'm definitely getting bad vibes about this."

"Oh, Robyn, cheer up," Nicole said. She gave her friend a playful shake. "Negative thoughts are bad for your immune system."

Alex grinned at her two girlfriends. They were such opposites. Nicole was always full of energy and usually in a good mood. Robyn was always predicting doom and gloom. Nicole was dark-skinned with big brown eyes and as quick to show righteous anger as she was to smile. Robyn was as pale as the moon, with long, straight red hair and green eyes that she often hid behind rose-colored granny glasses. Nicole was into issues and causes, rights and rebellions. Robyn wasn't into much besides the mall.

"Hey, guys! Wait up!" Louis Driscoll called out as he ran up to join the group. He and his family had just moved to Paradise Valley from Cincinnati, and he hung out a lot with Ray. "Boy, am I glad we're having an assembly."

"You, too?" Alex exclaimed. "How come?"

"Well, Madame Jones and I were having a little disagreement in French class. She wanted me to conjugate the verb *avoir*." He shrugged. "But I wanted to take *une petite* nap."

Ray laughed. "And what better place to take a nap than . . ."

"The auditorium during an assembly!" Louis and Ray said together.

Alex rolled her eyes. "Just promise me you guys won't snore like you did last time."

Suddenly Nicole's eyes widened. "Alex, look! Isn't that your mom? And look who she's with!"

Alex spun around.

Pushing through the heavy steel front doors of Danielle Atron Junior High School was . . .

Danielle Atron. She cleared a path in the sea of students like a shark swimming through a school of minnows.

Barbara Mack walked in right behind her, smiling as if she were about to pop. Alex knew something big was definitely up. Her mom was wearing her best plum-colored suit.

As Danielle stepped into the front office to announce her arrival, Alex hurried over to her mother. "Mom!" she exclaimed. "What are you doing here?"

Barbara Mack grinned. "Hi, honey. I'm working on a new project for Paradise Valley Chemical."

"But what's that got to do with school?"

"I'm sorry I couldn't tell you anything about it before, but Danielle made me promise to keep it a secret for a few days. You know how dramatic she likes to be about these things."

"I don't get it," Alex said.

"Danielle and I are going to make an announcement at the assembly," her mom explained. "Where will you be sitting? I'll look for you—"

"Barbara! Come!" Danielle strode past, her heels clicking loudly on the tile floor as she headed toward the auditorium. The vice principal trailed her like a hopeful puppy.

Barbara gave Alex a quick hug. "Gotta go, honey. Wave to me."

Alex stood in the middle of the hall staring at her mom as she ran off. Nicole finally yanked on the sleeve of Alex's blue plaid flannel shirt and asked, "What was that all about?"

Alex shook her head. "I have no idea."

Robyn groaned. "Danielle Atron's involved, so we know it's got to be trouble."

"Come on," Louis urged. "We gotta hurry. All the seats in the back are gonna be taken."

Alex and her friends hurried into the auditorium. But Alex didn't want to hang out in the back today. She wanted to sit closer to the front so she could see what her mom was up to. She led Robyn and Nicole down the aisle.

Sitting up on the stage, Alex's mom waved to her, then went back to discussing some note cards with Danielle.

"Well, where to?" Nicole asked.

Alex scanned the quickly filling rows. Then she grabbed Nicole's arm.

"There!"

Alex had found the perfect place, an aisle seat just a few rows down. It was near the front, with a good view of the stage. So what if it just happened to be right next to the most wonderful guy in the whole ninth grade? No, make that the whole school!

Scott Greene.

Beside her, Nicole nodded knowingly and gave Alex a little shove. "Go for it!"

Just then Scott turned around in his seat. When he saw Alex, he grinned and waved.

Alex smiled shyly. She used to be so nervous around Scott. Back when she was a seventh grader, she could hardly think of anything to say when he spoke to her. But she'd gotten over that, a little bit, anyway. And as she got to know him, she found she liked him even better. Now she knew that he was not only cute and smart and popular, he was also one of the nicest guys she'd ever met.

Alex straightened her baseball cap and headed toward the empty seat.

But someone shoved past her. "Is this seat taken?" the girl asked.

Alex stared as a tall, beautiful, ninth-grade girl slid into the seat next to Scott.

Kelly Phillips.

She looked as if she'd stepped from the pages of a fashion magazine. Perfect hair. Wonderful clothes. And a beauty-pageant smile.

With a sigh, Alex sank into a seat a few rows back. She watched in amazement as Kelly smoothly captured Scott's complete attention. "How does she do that?" Alex wondered aloud.

"Do what?" Nicole sat down beside her.

"Do what?" Robyn asked from two seats down.

Alex nodded toward Kelly. The girl had not stopped talking yet, or smiling. Scott seemed totally spellbound.

"Hypnosis?" Nicole joked.

"Witchcraft!" Robyn suggested.

Alex sighed. Even with all her powers, she didn't have half the power that Kelly seemed to have over Scott. "I'll never learn how to talk to boys like that. Never in a million years."

"What about me?"

Alex jumped in surprise and twisted around.

Behind her, Ray propped his chin on his hands on the back of her seat and grinned. "I'm a boy and you talk to me okay."

Louis poked his head in between Alex and Nicole. "What's this about boyfriends?" he asked in a voice loud enough to attract the attention of half the row in front of Alex. "Does Alex have a boyfriend? Or a secret crush? Come on, you can tell me!" Louis teased. At least five heads turned around, but luckily Scott and Kelly were too far away to hear.

Alex sank down into her seat as the row of faces in front of her all waited for her reply. How embarrassing! She felt the heat of a blush creep up her neck.

Uh-oh!

Quickly she ducked her head and buried her face in her hands. She hoped her long brown hair shielded the sides of her face.

She'd always hated that sensation—when a raging blush that she couldn't control broadcast her feelings to the whole world. But since she'd been doused with GC 161, it was even worse.

This was no ordinary blush. Her face was *glowing*. She could feel it, that tingling, throbbing sensation. Any time she got really nervous or embarrassed these days, her face glowed like some kind of mutant firefly. It was a weird side effect of the GC 161, totally unpredictable, and definitely the hardest to control.

Ray had seen her face this way dozens of times. But she couldn't let the others see it. As close as she was to Robyn and Nicole, she'd promised Annie she wouldn't tell them about her powers.

Remember what Annie says, Alex told herself. *Think of something else to stop glowing. Anything. Quick! . . . Two times two is four. Four times four is sixteen. . . . In 1492, Columbus sailed the ocean blue. . . . A-b-c-d-e-f-g . . .*

"Hey, you guys," Nicole said, leaning over the back of her seat, "I thought you were sitting in the back row."

"Nah," Louis said. "Too many geeks. We thought we'd sit up here and bother you."

Slowly Alex felt her face cool down. She peeked through her fingers at Scott and Kelly. Now she wished she *were* sitting in the back row so she wouldn't have to see Kelly in action. Alex couldn't help but watch her. Kelly tossed her hair like a model in a shampoo ad. She laid her hand on Scott's arm with practiced charm.

Scott laughed at something she said.

Kelly grinned like the Mona Lisa.

Who am I kidding? Alex thought to herself. *So Scott's nice to me. He's nice to everybody. But how could he ever think of her as special with someone like Kelly always hanging around?*

"Don't worry," Nicole whispered as she followed Alex's gaze. "Nobody can live on junk food forever," she teased.

Alex grinned. "What does that make me? Mashed potatoes and green beans?"

"Hey, there's nothing wrong with mashed potatoes and green beans! That's two major food groups."

"Gee, thanks, Nicole," Alex said. "Two out of four isn't bad, I guess."

Behind them, Louis said to Ray, "Are you having as much trouble following this conversation as I am?"

Finally the vice principal stepped up to the podium. "Testing. One, two, three." *Wrannnngg! Haaaannnngggg!*

Alex held her hands over her ears and laughed with her friends.

Frowning, the vice principal thumped the microphone with his finger. "Is this thing on? Can you hear me?" He cleared his throat directly into the microphone. "Students of Danielle Atron Junior High School, we are extremely honored today to have one of our town's most important citizens visit our school—our namesake, Ms. Danielle Atron." He paused to turn around and nod at Danielle.

Most of the teachers and a few kids clapped.

"Ms. Atron has an important announcement to make," the vice principal went on. "So I expect all of you to show her a warm Atron Junior High welcome."

The vice principal clapped loudly as he backed away. Alex and her friends clapped politely as Danielle stepped up to the lectern with a dazzling smile. She pulled some index cards from her jacket pocket and stacked them neatly on the podium.

"Good morning, children of Paradise Valley," Danielle began.

"Children?" Louis snorted. "Give me a break."

Alex and her friends snickered.

"I'm here today," she went on, "to announce a brand-new Paradise Valley Chemical community project, a project that will put the pride back into our community. We call it the Pick Up Paradise campaign!"

Grinning, Barbara Mack pointed to herself and mouthed to Alex, "I thought that up."

Danielle turned sharply and stared. Alex's mom quickly hid her grin and, with the vice principal's help, unrolled a huge green and gold banner that said PICK UP PARADISE and, in smaller letters underneath, KEEP PARADISE VALLEY CLEAN FOR THE CHILDREN—OUR FUTURE. They pinned the banner to the red curtain that stretched across the back of the stage.

Danielle smiled proudly and turned back to the students. "As part of the campaign," she added, "I am pleased to announce a contest—for you, the children of Paradise Valley."

Again the kids giggled.

"This is a great opportunity for all of you to show how much you love this beautiful town of ours," Danielle went on. "We invite you to develop projects that will clean up Paradise Valley and make our town more beautiful. Let's show all the world the pride we take in our community."

"Sounds like extra homework to me," Ray mumbled.

Danielle went on and on for a while about civic pride and Paradise Valley Chemical and pollution and litter.

Behind them, Louis made fake snoring sounds.

"Shhh!" Alex whispered, trying not to giggle. "You're going to get us all in trouble."

"To show our company's appreciation," Danielle concluded, "Paradise Valley Chemical will honor the top student projects during a special awards ceremony. And yes, there will be prizes! But prize or no prize, I am sure that each and every one of you will want to help 'Pick Up Paradise'! So get started today, and remember, we'll be watching. Thank you. And good luck!"

Danielle sat down. The vice principal returned to the podium. "Those students who wish to participate in the contest have permission to use school grounds in the afternoon to work on their projects. All projects will be judged on Tuesday the twenty-first, which is the week after next. We will have some forms in the office. Please fill these out in triplicate, have them signed by a parent and one of your teachers, and submit your project idea to the principal's office for approval. Good luck, everybody."

"See?" Ray said. "What'd I tell you? Homework!

The vice principal scanned the crowd. "Any announcements?"

The school nurse stood and reported that there was a virus going around with symptoms of sore throat, laryngitis, and fever. She reminded everyone of the best way to avoid getting sick: "Wash your hands with soap and warm water for at least fifteen seconds. That's about the time it takes to sing Happy Birthday. We don't want our students getting sick and missing school."

The head cafeteria lady stood up and said, "Contrary to the school menus published in the Sunday newspaper, there will be no fish sticks till Friday."

"Gee, what a bummer," Ray said sarcastically.

"I don't think I can go on living," Louis added.

"You know," Nicole said as they stood up to leave, "for once I agree with Danielle Atron. This Pick Up Paradise thing sounds like a good cause."

"I wonder what the prizes will be," Ray said.

Alex shrugged. "Maybe my mom will tell us."

As Alex moved toward the aisle, Scott suddenly

came up beside her and grinned. "Hey, Alex. Sounds pretty cool, huh? Gonna do a project?"

"Well . . . uh . . ." Alex hadn't really had time to think about it yet. But the way Scott was smiling at her made her make up her mind fast. "Yeah!" she said with a sudden smile.

Before she could say any more, Kelly came up and snaked her arm through Scott's. "Coming, Scott? We don't want to be late for class."

Then Kelly pretended to see Alex for the first time. "Oh, hi, Alex." She tucked a strand of her long brown hair behind her ear and stared at Alex's purple baseball cap, plaid flannel shirt, faded T-shirt, and baggy jeans. "What an original fashion statement," she added. Scott was too nice to notice her totally fake smile as she swept him off into the crowd.

"See you, Alex!" Scott called out over his shoulder.

In spite of Kelly's insult, Alex was beaming, because she'd just come up with a great idea. She'd found a way to solve all her problems.

Well, maybe not all of them. But a couple of important ones!

Her mind whirled with the possibilities. *I'll organize a fantastic project and win the Pick Up Paradise contest. Everybody in the whole school will know my name. Then Scott will realize I'm not just a nice little ordinary eighth grader! He might even—*

"Al-ex! Alex!"

She glanced toward the stage and saw her mom waving as she came down the steps.

Bonus points! Alex thought. *Just think how happy Mom and Dad will be if I win first place. For once they'll be proud of me. I'll bet my picture will even be in the newspaper. Even Annie will have to be impressed!*

Alex giggled as she imagined Annie's face when she had to listen to some grown-up say, "Oh, you must be Alex's big sister." Annie would finally understand what it was like to always be in someone's shadow.

Oh, wow! This is going to be great, Alex thought.

And the best part was she didn't need secret powers to pull it off.

"What's in it for me?" Ray asked as Alex and her friends walked home from school that afternoon.

Alex was trying to talk her friends into working on a Pick Up Paradise project with her. She'd gone by the main office at lunchtime and gotten entry forms for all of them.

"My dad's really coming down hard on me about my C in algebra," Ray went on. "I'm not sure I have time to work on a project that doesn't count toward school."

"But the cleanup campaign is for a good cause," Alex began. "Plus"—she grinned at Ray—"think how popular winning the contest will make us."

Ray smiled dreamily. "You're right. I'll be famous! Girls will be calling me for dates. I'll be a total babe magnet. One of them is bound to be able to help me with my math, too."

Everybody laughed.

"Well, I'm with Alex," Nicole said. "What's more important than cleaning up the earth?"

"Why bother?" Robyn moaned. "Have you seen the latest statistics on garbage? Every person in the United States throws out approximately four pounds of trash a day. And there's more than two hundred million people in the country. We're burying ourselves in the stuff. It's hopeless!"

"Come on, guys," Alex said. "It'll be great, especially if we all work together on a project. We're bound to come up with an idea that can win."

"I don't know, Alex," Robyn went on. "The teachers have really been piling on the homework lately. Besides, I'm fourteen years old, and in all my life I've never won anything."

"Well, count me in," Nicole said firmly. "I think this is a great way to get involved. Now is the time to wake up our consumeristic consciousness to the horrors of our throwaway lifestyle."

"I have no idea what she's talking about, but I'm in for sure," Ray said.

"What about you, Louis?" Alex asked.

"I don't know," Louis replied. "This crunchy-granola kind of Earth Day stuff—it's a little too small town for me, you know? Too low-tech. Back in Cincinnati I was used to doing things in a big way. I like major projects. I don't know if this little contest is the kind of thing I can sink my teeth into."

"How about a pizza planning party at my house tomorrow night?" Alex suggested. "Could you sink your teeth into that?"

Louis rubbed his stomach and thought a moment. "Uh, what time should I be there?"

"Let me check with my mom," Alex said, laughing. "I'll let you know."

She handed each of her friends three copies of the sign-up form. "Now, fill these out and bring them to the meeting. Be sure to get them signed by your parents. I expect every one of you to be there—with a whole bunch of ideas."

"All right, Alex!" Nicole exclaimed. "Taking charge."

Alex smiled sheepishly. "Sorry. I guess I'm just getting carried away." She shrugged. "But I really want to do this."

"Stop apologizing!" Nicole insisted. "I meant it

as a compliment. I like this attitude. It could be a whole new you."

"Hey, what's wrong with the old her?" Ray asked. "I like Alex the way she is."

Alex grinned. Good old Ray, just like a brother.

Nicole was such a good friend, too. She was always supportive, always encouraging Alex.

Was she right? Could this be the start of a whole new Alex Mack?

CHAPTER 4

When Alex got home, she poked her head into the garage to see if her sister was there.

The Macks didn't park cars in their garage. It was too full of junk, the washer and dryer, and Annie's experiments. She did most of her scientific research here, including her secret experiments on Alex and her unusual powers.

Today Annie was huddled over some kind of test-tube tower, with her nose about two inches from a beaker of gurgling green liquid.

"Hi, Annie. What ya doin'?"

Annie kept her eyes glued to the tubes. She added two drops of a blue liquid, and the contents of the test tube fizzed, which seemed to delight her. She didn't appear to know Alex was in the room.

Alex had learned a long time ago that when Annie was absorbed in a project, she forgot the rest of the world even existed, and she hated being interrupted. Since she was so smart in science, she found it hard to understand how other people might not be totally thrilled by it. After all, their father, George Mack, was a brilliant scientist, too, who worked in research and development at Paradise Valley Chemical.

"Yo, Annie, what are you up to?" Alex tried again.

"I'd tell you, Alex, but I don't think you'd understand," Annie said as she scribbled something in a notebook.

Even though Alex knew her sister wasn't trying to be mean, it usually hurt her feelings when Annie said stuff like that. But not today.

"I've got some big news!" she informed her sister.

"Oh, yeah?" Annie mumbled, still not taking her eyes off the experiment. "Like what? Did they close the junior high for lack of interest?"

"Sorry," Alex said mysteriously, "but I'm saving my news for the dinner table." Then she grabbed her basketball, made a face at Annie's back, and ran out to the driveway to shoot baskets till her mom and dad got home.

She dribbled. She jumped. Swish!

"All right!" Alex cheered, pumping the air with

her fist. She was up. She was feeling great. And she was going to score big time tonight with her news.

Alex waited till everyone had passed around the tossed salad and the vegetable lasagna.

"Guess what?" she said, grinning.

George Mack had a faraway look on his face as he reached for a roll. "Annie, did you see that article in *Scientific American* about the latest genetic research on—"

"George!"

Mr. Mack blinked. "Yes, dear?"

Barbara Mack gave him a look. Mr. Mack was just as absorbed in his work as Annie was in hers. Mrs. Mack often said he was so oblivious that she wondered how he found his way back home after work.

"I think Alex has something to tell us, George."

"Oh?" He put down his fork and turned to Alex. "I'm sorry, Alex," he said with affection. "What is it?"

"Yeah, Alex," Annie said. "What's the big news? Should we alert the media?"

Everyone stared at Alex, waiting.

Alex smiled proudly. "I'm going to win the Pick Up Paradise contest at school."

Annie snickered. "Alex, don't you think you should come up with a project before you decide where to put your award?"

"Now, Annie ..." Barbara Mack shot her older

daughter a warning glance, then smiled at her younger girl. "Alex, I like your confidence, and I think it's just great that you're doing a project. It's almost as if we'll be working together."

Alex gave Annie a satisfied smile.

"So how did you get involved in this, anyway, Mom?" Annie asked. "I thought you weren't so crazy about working with Danielle anymore."

"Well, I admit she's not the easiest person to work for," Mrs. Mack said. "Believe me, whenever I can do it without offending her, I try to pass her projects on to somebody else at the office. And I know she's just doing this Pick Up Paradise campaign to polish her image and get some good publicity for Paradise Valley Chemical."

"Now, Barbara," George Mack said, "Paradise Valley Chemical generates a lot of its own publicity because of the exciting things we're doing there in research and development. The work I'm heading up on GC 161 indicates that we may be very close to a major breakthrough."

Annie and Alex exchanged nervous glances.

"Uh, Dad," Annie asked. "Have they told you yet what GC 161 is?"

"Well . . ." Mr. Mack cleared his throat. "Not exactly. But that's because it's so important. The research is all very hush-hush. But we do know that GC 161 has some amazing properties. The word is that it could lead to a product, or products, that could benefit millons of people."

Alex giggled, and Annie shot her a warning glance. Once, while snooping in Danielle Atron's office, Annie had discovered what the company was trying to develop with GC 161: a diet pill that would allow people to stuff their faces and still not gain weight.

Mrs. Mack said with an affectionate grin, "You know we're very proud of you and your work at the company, George." She poured herself more ice water. "My point is that, yes, I know Danielle is just sponsoring this cleanup day for her own purposes. But who cares? The environment's a big issue with me. And for once she's paying me to work on a project with some guts in it, something that can really make a difference instead of just the usual fluff stuff."

"So, Alex," Mr. Mack said, "what kind of project are you doing? Anything I can help you with?"

Alex shook her head as she swallowed the last of her skim milk. "Thanks, Dad. But the rules say we have to do it on our own. No help from parents. And we haven't actually decided yet what we want to do."

"We?" Annie asked.

"Yeah—Robyn, Nicole, Ray, and Louis. Anyway, that's what I wanted to ask you," Alex said to her mom and dad. "Would it be okay if my group meets here tomorrow night for pizza? We need to work on our ideas for the project."

"It's okay with me," Annie said. "I won't be here."

"That's right," Mr. Mack said. "Annie and I are going to a lecture at the university."

"Well, it's fine with me," Mrs. Mack said. She gave Alex's hand a pat. "I'm really proud of you for taking an interest in this, Alex."

"Me, too," her dad said. "Good luck with your project."

"Thanks, Mom. Thanks, Dad."

Alex beamed. She couldn't remember when she'd last been the center of attention at the dinner table. And she hadn't even started the project yet! *I knew this was a good idea,* she thought happily. *It's going to be great!*

As Annie and Alex got up to take their dishes into the kitchen, Annie teased, "Yeah, good luck, Alex. Just don't let any of the judges see your side of the room!"

"What do you mean?"

"What do I mean?" Annie stared at her sister. "Disorganized Alex, Queen of the Messiest Room in Paradise Valley, is going to organize a winning cleanup project?" Annie shook her head and laughed.

Annie ducked as Alex threw a dish towel at her.

"Just wait, Annie!" Alex cried out. "I'll show you. You're not the only one who can win awards around here."

"Come on, Alex, I was only kidding," Annie said. "Hey, Alex, wait—"

The kitchen door swished as Alex ran upstairs.

"That Annie. She thinks she knows everything," Alex muttered under her breath.

Alex shoved open the door to her bedroom. Annie's perfect side looked as if a maid had just left. The rays of the setting sun slanting through the window glinted off Annie's framed awards. Alex felt like jumping on her sister's wrinkle-free bedspread, dumping her organized drawers on the floor, messing up her perfect desk.

But she didn't, of course.

Instead, she dumped her backpack to the floor, flopped down on her own cozy rumpled bed, and yanked her pillow over her head.

Think, Alex. Think! she told herself. *Wake up, brain! Time to go to work!*

She had to come up with some ideas. Some awesome ideas. Something that would snag the award and let everybody know that she was not just Annie Mack's boring little sister anymore.

She was somebody, too.

CHAPTER 5

"Did you think of anything yet?" Ray asked Alex as they walked to school the next morning.

"Nope," Alex said. "Well, that's not exactly true. I did come up with a few ideas."

"Yeah?"

"Yeah." Alex made a face. "Unfortunately they were all so stupid that I'm trying to forget them."

"Oh." Ray slung his arm across Alex's shoulders. "Don't worry, Al. I've got plenty of ideas. Just take your pick."

Alex broke into a smile. "Really, Ray? Oh, that's great. What? Tell me!"

He pulled a rumpled sheet of notebook paper out of his backpack and smoothed it out. "Let's see here. . . . We could make a giant model of the earth out of cafeteria garbage."

"Eww!"

"How about if we start a 'Bring Your Own Reusable Plate and Cup to School for Lunch' campaign? Or make volleyball nets out of the plastic rings from soda six-packs? Or get everyone in town to cut back to one bath a week to save water?"

Alex stuffed her hands into her pockets. "No, uh-uh, and forget it!"

"Oh, well, I'll think of something. We all will. That pizza tonight will jump-start our brains. Especially if it has pepperoni on it." Ray crumpled his list and tossed it into a trash can. "Oh, my dad said I could bring the soda, okay?"

"Sure. Thanks, Ray."

They walked along in silence for a while, till they crested the hill that looked down over the sprawling buildings of Danielle Atron Junior High.

Alex's face brightened. "Hey, what are we worried about? You know how the kids at school are. Half of them won't even bother to enter because they don't have to. We probably won't have much competition."

"I'll bet you're right," Ray said. "We'll blow them all away."

But as they headed into the school, Alex got a sinking feeling in the pit of her stomach.

A normal morning at Danielle Atron Junior High looked like this: kids yawning, kids daydreaming on the way to homeroom, kids hanging out by lockers gossiping about kids at other lockers.

But not this morning.

First of all, everybody looked wide awake—except for Rodney van Winkle. He never really woke up until the final bell rang in the afternoon.

Second of all, everyone seemed excited.

"What's going on? Do you think the teachers are on strike?" Alex asked Ray.

"Maybe the health department closed down the cafeteria," Ray suggested.

Alex and Ray caught snatches of conversation as they moved down the hall to their lockers:

"Wait till I tell you my idea. . . ."

"My dad said he can help us. . . ."

"We're having a meeting after school. Can you stay?"

This was totally weird.

Maybe it was spring fever. Maybe it was that article in *Slash* magazine about Earth Day. Who knew?

But it seemed as if every kid at Danielle Atron Junior High was doing a Pick Up Paradise project. Uh-oh!

Robyn was waiting for Alex at her locker.

"Hi, Robyn," Alex said as she worked her combination.

Robyn leaned back against the lockers with a look

of total gloom on her face. "Cancel tonight's meeting, Alex."

"Cancel it?"

"There is no way we can win now," Robyn declared. *"Everybody's* doing a project."

"Ignore her," Nicole insisted, suddenly appearing on Alex's other side. "Stiff competition is good for us. It's what pumps us up!"

"Yeah, pumps us up for a big fall," Robyn grumbled.

"Robyn! Come on, now," Nicole said. "You can't win if you don't believe you can win."

"Well, I don't. My motto is 'Expect the worst. Then you'll never be disappointed.' "

Alex leaned against her locker and rubbed her eyes. She felt a headache coming on—a big one, right in the center of her brain where all those fabulous ideas ought to be.

She'd dreamed about winning the contest the night before. The kids in the audience had cheered and given her a standing ovation—well, her and the rest of her group, too. Scott had rushed onstage to hand her a huge armful of red roses. Then, with that crooked smile of his, he'd leaned over to give her a congratulatory kiss when—

Annie had thrown a pillow at her to wake her up. Annie always ruined the best dreams.

Alex sighed and pulled out books for first and

second period as she listened to Robyn and Nicole debate the pros and cons of a positive attitude.

Maybe it was hopeless. Maybe the project wasn't worth all the effort if there was no way they could win.

Alex glanced up. Scott was across the hall, taking a drink from the water fountain.

Before she knew what she was doing, Alex hurried over to the water fountain. She stood there, hugging her books.

Scott straightened up and grinned when he saw her. "Hey, Alex."

"Hi, Scott."

Well, don't just stand there, she told herself. *Ask him!*

"Um, a couple of my friends and I are going to work on a Pick Up Paradise project together. We're meeting tonight for pizza, at my house. You know, to work on it. I was wondering . . . Would you like to come?"

Scott smiled. "I'd love to, Alex—"

"You would?"

"Well, I would, but—"

"But he can't."

Alex cringed as Kelly walked up and sort of wedged herself into the conversation. She smiled sweetly. "Scott already volunteered to work on my project. Didn't you, Scott?"

Scott shrugged and nodded.

"Didn't you see my poster, Alex?" Kelly pointed to the bulletin board across the hall. A bunch of kids had gathered around a poster, which they were reading. The poster said:

Kelly Phillips says:
"BE THERE OR BE SQUARE"
Help Create the Winning
Pick Up Paradise Project
Time: 3:30 P.M.
Place: Ms. Buncombe's room

"I'd invite you to join our group, too," Kelly added.

"Well, I don't—" Alex began.

"But I'm sure you'd rather do something with your eighth-grade friends," Kelly added in a rush. "Oh, and Alex, I just love your little hat, by the way. Wherever did you find it? It's so . . . unusual. Come on, Scott. We gotta go."

Alex watched them walk away. She was definitely in a "Robyn" mood after seeing Kelly. Now she knew why the whole school was buzzing. They weren't excited about their own projects; most of them were excited about working on Kelly's project. Now Alex would be competing with the whole school. And how could she possibly impress Scott with her project when he was going to be working on some awesome project with Kelly?

If only she knew what kind of project Kelly was planning. Then she might have a chance to beat her. But how could she find out?

Alex glanced back at the bulletin board. Kelly's meeting was at three-thirty, in Ms. Buncombe's room. Suddenly an idea popped into Alex's head. Maybe she could be there after all. . . .

That afternoon after school, Alex and Ray met at her locker. She'd explained her plan—and said that she might need his help. They waved good-bye to Robyn, Nicole, and Louis. "See you at my house at six," she reminded them. "And come loaded with ideas!"

Then Alex and Ray hung around her locker, killing time. Down the hall she could see kids showing up for Kelly's meeting in Ms. Buncombe's room.

Alex waited until everyone was inside. Then she motioned for Ray to follow her as she slowly, casually, strolled toward the room.

She and Ray pretended to look at the announcements on the bulletin board near the door to Ms. Buncombe's room. But actually Alex was concentrating her hardest on trying to hear what Kelly's group was discussing.

Slam!

Alex jumped. Kelly had slammed the door. On

the other side of the glass in the door's window, she stood there smiling her fake smile at Alex. Then she waved good-bye and placed a big piece of poster board over the glass, so that no one could see in. On the paper it said: Top-secret Meeting— Keep Out!

Alex pressed her ear to the door.

"Can you hear anything?" Ray whispered.

Alex shook her head. "I can hear voices—mostly Kelly's. But I can't make out what anybody is saying."

Alex couldn't peek in, either, because the small square window was completely covered with the poster board.

Alex had Ms. Buncombe for fifth period, so she knew what the room looked like. "Time for Plan B," Alex whispered to Ray. "Come on!"

Together they dashed outdoors and around the building. When they reached the windows of Ms. Buncombe's classroom, they ducked behind some bushes.

Alex dropped her backpack to the ground and peeked in through the window. Kelly was up front, talking and smiling and waving her arms around. The rest of the kids, including Scott, sat with their backs to the window. Just to Alex's right there was an aquarium on top of some bookshelves. The window was open about an inch.

Perfect.

Alex glanced around the school yard. Some kids were hanging out by the bike racks. *Go home!* she silently ordered. She waited until they unlocked their bikes, yakked awhile, then rode off.

At last the grounds appeared to be empty. "Okay, Ray. Cover me!"

"Gotcha," Ray whispered back, then muttered to himself, "This is so cool!"

Alex grinned and got ready. Annie would be furious with her if she knew what she was about to do. "That was totally unnecessary, Alex!" Annie would probably say. "Somebody could have seen you. What were you thinking?"

Alex was going to do it anyway.

She was going to morph. She used to be totally terrified of changing into a liquid. Who wouldn't be? It was scary. Now that she'd done it dozens of times, she was a little more used to it. But she still went through a few moments of serious fear. After all, what if this time she got stuck as a puddle and couldn't turn back into a girl?

Annie had done all kinds of experimenting on Alex's liquefying abilities. She said she was beginning to believe that Alex would always be able to change back to her normal human form. But she wasn't a hundred percent certain.

Alex glanced around to make sure no one was watching.

Ray gave her a thumbs-up sign.

Alex closed her eyes and stood as still as she could. She thought of water—rivers, lakes, and rain. Gradually she began to tingle, and her head grew dizzy, as if it were full of soda bubbles.

Then, in a flash, she was sinking into herself, like she was melting, but without heat. The next thing she knew, she was a puddle of thick silvery liquid about the size of a bath mat.

Ray let out the breath he'd been holding and looked down at the gelatinous silver puddle on the grass. "Wow!" he whispered. "Alex, I don't think I'll ever get used to seeing you do that. It's awesome."

Alex's laugh came out as a gurgle. But it was now time to get down to business. In the past when she morphed, she'd only been able to stay in her liquid form for about five minutes, so she'd have to hurry.

Mentally, Alex willed herself to move forward. Like a cross between a jellyfish and a snake, she climbed the outside wall of the school, flowed over the windowsill, and seeped through the open window.

Once inside, she slithered up the glass wall of the aquarium and plopped in with a soft splash.

For a moment Kelly stopped talking. Alex froze in place and watched her. Kelly frowned as she glanced curiously at the back of the room. But after a moment she shrugged and went on.

Alex stifled a giggle as she floated on top of the

cold, slightly slimy water. The fish in the tank were zipping back and forth, totally freaked out. Alex lay still, allowing the water to calm. After a moment, the fish must have realized she wasn't going to hurt them, and they went back to their normal business of swimming in circles and making kissy faces in the glass.

Now Alex could see and hear everything perfectly.

She listened to Kelly talk for a moment, then quickly realized that this wasn't a meeting for Kelly's group to come up with an idea after all. Kelly had already decided on the project she wanted to do. Her goal today was to sign people on and split up the work.

A few kids grumbled a little about that, but not too many. Kelly was an expert at seeming really nice while she was getting her own way. Plus—Alex had to admit—Kelly's idea was great.

They were going to build a big billboard with the Pick Up Paradise slogan on it, and put it up where the whole town would see it. It sounded flashy, too, with lights and motors and moving parts. Everyone who worked on it would get his or her name printed along the bottom. The kids really liked that.

"Won't that be wonderful?" Kelly said with a glowing smile. "It will be a permanent reminder to the residents of Paradise Valley not to litter."

And, Alex thought ruefully, a permanent reminder of how wonderful Kelly was. Everyone who passed it would think of Kelly.

Suddenly Alex felt a weird tingling. *Oops! Better get out of here—fast,* she thought. It would be pretty embarrassing to suddenly morph back to normal right then. Wouldn't Kelly just love to find her sitting in a fish tank at the back of the room.

Quickly Alex sloshed out of the tank, then oozed out the window and down the wall.

She waited a moment, lying on the cool grass, for Ray to give her an okay.

"All clear," Ray hissed. "Do your stuff."

Alex concentrated. She filled her mind with an image of herself, as if she were looking in a mirror. The fizzy bubbles swept over her once more, and suddenly she was standing next to Ray in the same clothes she'd been wearing before.

"And you're not even wet!" Ray shook his head in admiration.

Even Annie the brain hadn't been able to figure that one out yet! Alex didn't fret about it too much, though. She was just glad that was how it worked.

"How do I look, Ray?" she asked with a slightly nervous laugh. "Everything back in the right place?"

Ray squinted at her, then reached out to yank her right ear. "Except for that extra ear, you look great."

"Ray!"

"I'm kidding. You're fine."

Alex picked up her backpack and slung it over her shoulder. But before she could step out from the bushes, the window behind her slammed open.

"Alex Mack! What are you doing?"

Alex gulped and glanced at Ray. Slowly they turned around.

Kelly!

How much had she seen?

Then Scott looked out, too, with a puzzled expression on his face. "Hi, Alex. Hi, Ray. What's up?"

"N-nothing," Alex said, slowly backing away. "Um, one of my test papers blew out of my hand. I thought maybe the wind blew it behind these bushes."

"Come on, Alex," Ray said as he grabbed her arm. "Let's look over by the bike racks."

"Hope you find it," Scott called out, then ducked back inside.

Kelly didn't say anything. But she folded her arms, and her eyes narrowed as she watched Alex and Ray dash off.

"Whew! That was close!" Ray gasped as they race-walked across the school grounds. When they were two blocks from school, they finally slowed down.

When she'd caught her breath, Alex told Ray everything she'd heard about Kelly's project, how it would have everybody's name on it and be placed where the whole town could see it. "A billboard is pretty flashy," she finished.

Ray nodded. "It will definitely get noticed."

"But is it the kind of project that will win the contest?" Alex kicked at an aluminum can that was lying on the ground. It rolled noisily along the cement sidewalk.

"We've got to think of something better," she muttered. She came to the can again and gave it another kick.

Clink-clink-clink!

"Something cool enough to beat a flashy billboard."

Clink-clink-clink!

"Something . . ."

Alex stopped. Frowning, she pulled a grape-colored bandanna out of her pocket and wrapped it around her hand. Then she picked up the can, jogged to the corner, and slam-dunked the can in the trash.

Alex looked up and down the street. "This is such a beautiful neighborhood," she said to Ray. "I can't believe people are so lazy! What kind of person would just throw trash right on the ground when there's a trash can nearby?"

"Beats me," Ray said.

Shaking her head, Alex said, "Somebody should do something about it."

CHAPTER 6

"Alex! You've been robbed!" Louis cried, looking frantically around her bedroom. "Somebody came in here and totally trashed this place. Quick. Give me the phone and I'll call the police!"

Alex, Nicole, and Robyn crossed their arms and stared at Louis. Ray fell on the bed laughing.

"Yeah, well, I'd like to see your room," Alex remarked. Glancing around her room, she said, "What's the big deal, anyway? It looks okay to me. I even tried to clean up a little before you guys got here." There wasn't a single dirty sock on the floor. There was even room for all of them to sit down.

Alex thought Louis was a pretty nice guy. Most of the time he was even kind of funny. But sometimes his joking around got a little—how should she put it?—obnoxious!

Louis sat down on Annie's bed and wiped his eyes, he was laughing so hard. He looked around. "Hey, did your sister go away to college already?"

Alex frowned, puzzled. "No . . ."

Louis stopped laughing. "You mean her side of the room looks this neat all the time?" he exclaimed. He ran his hand along the nightstand. "Wow! I never saw anything like it."

"Forget Annie, okay?" Alex snapped. "Now, come on. The pizza should be here any minute. Let's get started."

Ray and Robyn sat on the floor. Nicole sat on the bed next to Alex, and Louis sat on the chair by Annie's desk.

"I hereby nominate Alex as chairman of this project committee," Nicole said, slapping Alex on the back.

Ray's hand shot up. "I second it. All in favor?"

"Aye!" they all said at once.

Nicole grinned. "Congratulations, Alex. You're officially in charge."

"And officially responsible for any problems, headaches, troubles, or fines," Robyn added.

Alex blinked, her mouth hanging open. "Well," she said with a shaky laugh, "I guess that's one thing settled. Thank you for your vote of confidence."

Cool! Alex thought. She had never actually been the chairman of a committee before. It was a big responsibility.

She opened up a spiral notebook and uncapped a purple felt-tipped pen. "Okay," she said. "Any ideas?"

No one said anything.

"Not any? What have you guys been doing?"

"Try homework," Robyn said.

"Chores," Ray said.

"Baby-sitting," Nicole said.

"Ultimate Frisbee game," Louis said.

"And playing the horn," Ray added.

"How about you, Alex?" Louis asked. "Let's hear your ideas."

"Well . . ." Alex stalled. She hated to admit it. She didn't have a single one!

Just then Annie tapped on the door and stepped into the room, holding three big pizza boxes. "Alex, your pizzas are here. When's the football team showing up?"

Ray jumped up and grabbed the boxes. "Don't worry! We promise not to leave any leftovers."

"By the way, Alex, I've got something for you." Annie crossed to her desk and pulled some books from her shelf. "Here," she said, handing them to Alex. "These might help."

Alex stared at the books. They were all about Earth Day, the environment, and recycling. She glanced up at her sister in surprise. "Gee, thanks, Annie."

Annie shrugged. "Hey, I figure you guys need all the help you can get," she teased. "See you later. Mom's working in her room. Dad and I won't be back from our lecture till late."

The group of kids moved into the kitchen, where Ray passed out cold cans of soda while Louis ripped open the first pizza box. At the table, the girls began to flip through the books Annie had given them. They were packed with ideas for the three R's: Reduce, Reuse, and Recycle.

"Wow, I didn't know all this stuff," Alex said. "Like the fact that a ten-minute shower uses less water than a bath."

"Or that kids could save trees by carrying lunch to school in reusable containers instead of paper bags, sandwich bags, or foil," Nicole added.

Robyn was spellbound by a book that gave statistics on just how bad the pollution problem really was. "Whoa! It says here that packaging accounts for three out of every ten barrels of trash."

Nicole nodded. "My mom is really big on that. She carries her own tote bags to stores. And she goes out of her way to choose products that use the least amount of packaging."

"That's a great idea," Alex said. "I'm going to start doing that."

"Speaking of great ideas, Alex, you were about to tell us your great ideas for the project," Louis said. He made a loud slurping noise as he finished his can of soda. He crushed the can with a macho grunt, then tossed it all the way across the kitchen into a trash can in the corner.

Clink!

"Louis!" Robyn snapped, looking up from her book. "I can't believe you did that."

"Neither can I," Ray said, shaking his head in admiration. "Great aim, Louis."

"Thanks. Come on. Try yours, Ray."

Ray squinted, took aim, shot—

Clink!

"All right! Three points!" Louis shouted with both fists in the air.

"No, no, no. That's not what I was talking about," Robyn said. "I meant I can't believe you threw your soda can in the trash."

"What am I supposed to do? Eat it?" Louis asked.

"Why not?" Ray said. "You eat everything else! Let me tell you, girls, this guy has an iron stomach."

Nicole held up her book and shook it. "It says right here that that aluminum can you just threw away will still be here, in the city dump, five hundred years from now."

"Incredible . . ." Louis said slowly. "Really?"

"And look at this," Alex added. "We throw away almost four million tons of office paper every year. And almost ten million tons of newspapers."

"Somebody should do something about this," Robyn murmured as she flipped a page.

Alex remembered the litter she'd often seen by the side of the road on the way to school, like the aluminum can she'd picked up on the street on her way home. And she thought about what Robyn had just said: *"Somebody should do something about this."* It was the same thing Alex had said that afternoon.

And maybe I'm that somebody, Alex thought.

"Okay," she said.

"Okay, what?" Nicole asked.

"Okay, let's do something about it."

Her friends looked at her, waiting for more. First she told them what she'd heard about Kelly's billboard idea.

"Oooh, that's good," Nicole admitted.

"Too good," Robyn moaned.

"I wonder who's working on the mechanics," Louis said.

"Wait! I admit it's glitzy," Alex said. "But it's still just something to look at. There's no guarantee that it will change what people do." She jumped up and began to pace. "What we need to do is get people involved—really *do* something about the litter problem in this town."

Louis ripped into the last box of pizza. "Like what?"

"There's a story in this book about a group that did a 'Clean Sweep' in their community. Why don't we do the same thing?" Alex said excitedly. "We can choose some sites in town where there's a lot of litter and get kids at school to help clean it up."

Alex flipped through the book. "We'll need some supplies, though. Garbage bags and work gloves. Let's go into my room and get some paper to make a list."

Everyone grabbed their slices and headed upstairs.

"All this stuff will cost money," Robyn said, when they'd settled back in the bedroom.

"Well, we can think up some way to raise money for supplies," Alex said.

"Like a bake sale?" Ray said.

"Can anybody here cook?" Louis asked skeptically.

"Microwave brownies," Robyn said. "That's about it."

"I'm not sure how much that would raise," Alex said. She picked up a T-shirt from her desk chair and sat down. The shirt was one her mom had brought her from a business trip to New York City. It said GET DOWN TO BUSINESS.

"Hey, maybe we could sell T-shirts!" Alex said. "You know, like with the Pick Up Paradise slogan printed on them. The profits could go to buying the supplies we need. And kids can wear the shirts on the cleanup day, too."

"The day of the pickup, we can also sort out anything that can be recycled, like aluminum cans and bottles," Nicole said.

"Sounds like a lot of work," Robyn said.

"Well, I like it," Nicole said. "What do you guys think? Do you want to do the cleanup?"

Louis was hunched over another book. "Nope."

"Why not?" Alex asked.

"Goats!"

Alex and her friends exchanged blank glances. "Goats?"

"Yeah. Look, Ray. What do you think?" Louis was looking at one of Alex's books, titled *Welcome to Switzerland*, which she'd checked out of the library for a geography report. He had it open to a picture of mountain goats grazing on a hillside in the Alps.

Ray scratched his head. "I don't get it."

"It'll be great," Louis said. "You know how in old cartoons goats are always eating garbage, like tin cans and stuff? We're going to bring that idea into the nineties. Goats Against Garbage! Hey, that's GAG for short."

"Brilliant," Ray said. "We can do a project show-ing how goats can clean up all the garbage and litter in town—and then turn it into fertilizer."

"Wait a minute, wait a minute," Alex said. "Goats don't really eat garbage like that, do they? I think that's just some old myth."

"Hey," Ray deadpanned, "if it's in cartoons, it must be true. Right, Louis?"

He and Louis laughed and high-fived. Then they grabbed a sheet of paper from Annie's desk and started making notes on the cost and manpower in-volved in using a small army of goats to graze along the roadside and eat up all the litter.

"And what about letting the goats do all the yard work?" Ray suggested.

"Yeah! We can use 'em to mow the lawn, too!" Louis exclaimed. "Double project. A pollution-free answer to a guy's most aggravating problem."

Robyn rolled her eyes. "Give me a break."

"Do you believe these guys?" Nicole said to Alex.

Alex wasn't sure how it had happened, but she felt as if she'd totally lost control of the meeting. She picked up a shoe off the floor and banged it on the corner of her desk. "I call this meeting to order now! Come on, guys. Quiet!"

Her friends settled down.

"Okay, let's put it to a vote," Alex said. "All in favor of selling T-shirts and sponsoring a Pick Up Paradise cleanup day, raise your right hand."

Alex raised her hand. So did Nicole and Robyn.

Ray and Louis sat with their hands folded in their laps. Alex waited for them to raise their hands, but they didn't move a muscle.

"Ray!" Alex said. "Louis, come on. Be serious! You don't really want us to do a project on goats, do you?"

The guys just nodded, grinning smugly.

"You can't be for real," Alex pleaded.

"We're not joking, Alex," Louis said. "Well, actually we are joking, a little," he admitted with a smirk. "I mean, what good is a project like this if we can't have a little fun with it?"

"But it's also got to be a serious project, not just a joke. And it's got to be better than Kelly's to win," Alex insisted. "My project can win—and it'll be fun, too."

"Oh, really?" Louis made a face. "Spending a day picking up somebody else's garbage? Thanks, but no thanks. I get enough of that kind of fun at home."

Alex folded her arms. She was the chairman—uh, chairwoman. And a chairwoman was supposed to take charge. "Well, if you're in this group, you have to do what the group wants to do. And the majority of us want to do a cleanup day."

Louis stood up. "No offense, Alex, but I think I want to do my own project. I hope that's cool with you. Maybe I can come to the cleanup day, too." Louis stood up and headed for the door. "Thanks for the pizza. I'll be seeing ya."

Ray got up to leave, too.

"Ray!" Alex exclaimed, jumping up to stop him. "You can't—"

"I just want to talk to Louis a minute," Ray said. With an apologetic shrug, he followed Louis out the door and down the stairs.

"Oh, great," Alex said. "I finally come up with a decent idea, something that might really win, and lose half my committee."

Nicole pulled Alex down beside her on the bed and handed her a cold slice of pepperoni pizza. "Forget them. Here. Eat. You haven't touched a bite."

Alex tore off a piece of crust and nibbled, but she suddenly wasn't very hungry.

Robyn sat down on the other side of Alex. "Let them go, Alex. If they're not into the project, they'll only bring us down anyway."

"Robyn's right," Nicole said. "Who needs them?"

"Okay." Alex sighed and began to fill out the project form for school. Nicole and Robyn helped

her get the wording just right. As Alex saw her
ideas taking shape on the paper, she started getting
excited again. *Yeah*, she thought. *This is a great idea,
and we can do it all by ourselves.*

"We'd better write down all the things we need
to do," Alex said, picking up her pad of paper. She
began to make a list.

Just then Alex heard someone coming up the
stairs. She looked at her watch. Annie wasn't due
home for at least another hour. Who could it be?

"Is this committee still in session?" Ray asked
from the doorway.

"Ray!" Alex exclaimed.

"Listen, Alex," Ray said quickly. "I'm sorry about
Louis and the goats and everything."

"That's okay," Alex said coolly.

"I really would like to work on the goats project,"
he added.

"Oh." Alex tried not to show how bummed she
felt.

"But I want to work on your project, too."

"Well," Robyn said. "Make up your mind. You
can't do both."

Ray grinned. "Why not?"

Alex stared at him.

"Who says you can work on only one project?"
Ray asked. "It's not in the rules or anything."

Alex thought it over. She knew Louis's goat project was mostly just for fun. It couldn't possibly win. And she really did want Ray's help.

"I move that this committee approves Ray Alvarado's membership on the project," Alex said. "Robyn? Nicole? What do you say?"

Robyn and Nicole whispered a moment. Then Nicole spoke: "The more the merrier! Let's get to work!"

Ray grinned as he sat down and grabbed his cold pizza crust, which he'd left behind.

"We're going to make a dynamite team," Nicole said.

"Watch out, Kelly!" Alex shouted. "Your billboard has finally met its match!"

CHAPTER 7

The next morning Alex sat at the breakfast table chewing toast and staring into space, thinking about her project.

Her dad was reading a scientific journal as he tried to spear his scrambled eggs without looking. Annie was eating cereal with one hand and copying notes from a textbook onto a pad.

Barbara Mack sipped coffee and attempted to chitchat with her oblivious family. "It's so nice for us to have this quality time together before we start our busy day," she said wryly.

No one seemed to hear her.

"So, Alex," her mom said, "how's your project coming?"

"Fine," Alex mumbled as she chewed.

"Oh. Do you have a project idea yet?"

"Uh-huh."

Mrs. Mack pursed her lips. "Well, would you like to tell us about it?"

Alex glanced at the clock. "Oops! Can't. Gotta go. Bye, Mom. Bye, Dad. Bye, Annie."

Mrs. Mack groaned.

"Did you say something, dear?" Mr. Mack said without looking up as he underlined a paragraph in his magazine.

Alex grabbed her backpack and headed toward the door.

At lunchtime Alex, Ray, Nicole, and Robyn met in the cafeteria to discuss their plans.

"We need to divide up the tasks," Alex said, writing the words "To do" at the top of a piece of paper.

Robyn dunked a limp french fry into a puddle of ketchup. "Maybe we should decide what the tasks are first."

"Okay," Alex said, thinking. "First . . . Hmm."

"Maybe the first thing we should do is pick a site to pick up," Nicole suggested.

"Good idea," Alex said, and wrote down "Place."

They all thought for a few minutes.

"How about my garage?" Ray joked. "Or Alex's room?"

Alex pretended to glare at her friend.

They all thought some more.

"I know!" Alex said. "What about that huge empty meadow between the Welcome to Paradise Valley sign and the park? I've seen a lot of litter there."

"Good idea," Nicole said.

"I agree," Robyn said. "It's really gross there."

Alex wrote down "Meadow near welcome sign."

"Maybe we should make some posters," Ray suggested. "You know, telling people to come to the cleanup."

Alex wrote down "Posters," then suggested, "How about if we each make four or five posters and find places to put them up?"

Everyone agreed. They discussed what to put on the posters and decided to hold the cleanup a week from Saturday. That would be the last weekend to hold it before Danielle Atron came to school to judge the projects.

Nicole stirred her blueberry yogurt thoughtfully. "I think I'd like to see if some business in town would donate the work gloves."

"Good thinking," Alex said. "That will keep down our expenses."

"Hey, maybe I could sell lemonade on the day of the cleanup," Ray said. "People will probably get thirsty. We might make a lot of money that way."

"Great!" Alex was growing more and more excited as she wrote on her pad. Ideas were really flowing now. Their project was going to be terrific.

"Next order of business: T-shirts," Alex said.

"I know where we should go," Robyn said. "There's a place on the way home called Talkin' Tees and Cheap Copies."

She and Alex decided to go there that afternoon after school.

Alex finished her tuna sandwich as she looked over her list. "This looks good," she announced. "Ray, do you think—"

"Ray!" Louis hurried over to the table. He quickly said hi to everyone, then said, "Listen, Ray. There's a book about goats in the library you've got to see, but it's a reference book and the librarian won't let me check it out. Come on. We still have a few minutes before the bell rings."

Ray stood and picked up his tray. "I guess I gotta go, guys. Alex, I'll see you later, okay?"

"But, Ray—"

Louis was already dragging Ray toward the trash cans, talking a mile a minute. Alex frowned. She reminded herself that she had to be fair. Ray had promised to help Louis with his project, too.

But somehow that didn't make her feel any better.

After school Alex and Robyn went to Talkin' Tees and Cheap Copies, a local copy shop that also did small print jobs like bumper stickers and T-shirts.

As Alex pushed open the door, a tiny bell rang

and a guy with a long dark ponytail and a mustache looked up from the counter. He was wearing a tie-dyed T-shirt that said VISUALIZE WHIRLED PEAS.

"Can I help you, ladies?" the man said. A tiny name tag pinned to his shirt said Roger.

"We'd like to order some T-shirts," Alex said.

"You've come to the right place," Roger said. "T-shirts are my life." He grabbed a clipboard and wrote the date on an order form. "Just fill this out. I'll need to know how many shirts you want, what sizes, what colors, whether you want one hundred percent cotton or a cotton-poly blend, and what you want the T-shirts to say. Got any graphics?"

"Uh, no," Alex said.

Roger handed Alex a sheet of hot-pink paper. "Here's our price list on a per-shirt basis. As you can see, the price drops a little the more shirts you order. Oh, and we require a fifty percent deposit."

Alex's head swam as she stared at the sheet of paper. She'd had no idea that ordering T-shirts would be so complicated. She hadn't even thought about most of these things. And the prices! Yikes! They were a lot higher than she expected.

"What do you think?" she whispered to Robyn. "How much money do you have?"

"On me?" Robyn dug into her pockets and came up with one dollar and thirty-seven cents.

"Not good. I'm pretty broke too. What are we going to do?"

Robyn shook her head and shrugged.

Alex took a big breath and stepped back to the counter. "We've never done this before," she said apologetically.

Roger smiled. "That's okay. I'm the expert; you're the customer. Let's start out simple. Tell me what the shirts are for."

Alex took a deep breath and told him all about the Pick Up Paradise contest and the project they were trying to do.

"To tell you the truth," Alex admitted, "I didn't realize that I might have to pay part of the money up front. I was planning to pay for them out of the profits we made, but I guess it makes sense that you need some money first."

Roger smiled. "I'll tell you what. Maybe we can work out a deal."

"What kind of deal?" Robyn asked suspiciously.

Roger laughed. "An honest deal. First of all, I'm hip to what you kids are doing. The environment is a big issue with me. I wasn't much older than you when we had the first Earth Day."

"Really?" Alex said. "But that was like . . . more than twenty-five years ago."

"You got it—1970. Man, those were the days! At my high school we wore gas masks and held a funeral for an old junked car to protest air pollution from auto exhaust. That was back when everybody's gasoline still had lead in it. Man, it was so far out! We had a great time."

"Wow," Alex said. She couldn't help but giggle. Roger was about the same age as her father, but they sure were different. She'd have to remember to ask her parents what they did on the first Earth Day.

"My kid goes to school at Atron Junior High, too," Roger said. "Maybe you know him—Sky Kapsalakis?"

Alex frowned. "We know a David Kapsalakis." David was tall, had extremely short hair, wore black-framed glasses, and dressed like an accountant.

"That's him!" Roger chuckled. "He switched to his middle name when we moved here about three years ago. But I'll never get used to calling him David. His mother named him Sky because his eyes were as blue as the sky. Still are."

"He looks just like you," Robyn said. Alex saw her cross her fingers behind her back.

"Thanks. Anyway, since this is for a good cause and you go to Atron Junior High and all, I'll cut a deal with you. I'll waive the deposit and knock two dollars off the price of each shirt if you'll give me a plug on your shirts. Just something little: 'T-shirts printed by Talkin' Tees' with the phone number in small type. Something like that. What do you say?"

"Just a minute," Robyn said. She took Alex aside. "If we say yes, does it mean we're selling out to big business?" she whispered.

"I don't think so," Alex whispered back. "I say let's do it."

Robyn nodded.

Alex walked back to the counter and stuck out her hand. "It's a deal!" This was her first executive decision. She wished Annie could see her in action. "And thanks a lot, Mr. Kapsalakis."

"No problemo!" Roger said. "And please, call me Roger. The word 'Mister' makes me feel old. By the way, I dig your groovy hat. Where'd you get it? I'd love to get Sky one in purple."

Alex tugged on her chocolate-colored crocheted hat. "Thanks. My mom got it for me on a trip."

Roger helped them fill out the order form. He even helped them pick out some cute clip art to go on the front of the shirts under the logo. The girls picked a drawing of two funky kids holding up the planet Earth, with their dog barking at it as if he wanted to play ball.

"Oh, and we need them by next Saturday," Alex remembered to say.

"Hmm. That'll be tight. I'm working on a big job for the Paradise Valley Chemical bowling league."

"Uh-oh," Alex said with a gulp. "I really need them by next Saturday."

Roger pulled on his mustache, then scribbled something on the form. "Not to worry. I'll have them by Friday at noon.

"We'll be here! And thanks again."

"You're welcome."

On Saturday Alex, Robyn, and Nicole made posters. Ray showed up late because he and Louis had been running around trying to find goats. They all spent the rest of the weekend putting posters up around town. Roger was more than happy to let them put one in his window at the T-shirt shop. They also saved several to hang at school.

On Monday Alex got permission from the principal to take orders for T-shirts at lunch and after school. Roger had made a sample T-shirt with their design on it to show the kids.

By the end of the day, Alex was surprised and delighted—a lot of kids ordered shirts. She got money for the T-shirts up front, so that she had plenty of money for supplies. She planned to pass out the shirts on the day of the cleanup.

Alex and her friends took turns selling shirts on Tuesday. The only problem was that Ray showed up late during his lunch period, explaining that he had to do something for Louis's project.

"Ray, are you with us or not?" Alex finally asked him after lunch on Tuesday. "We really need your help."

"I'm sorry, Alex," he said. "I promise I'll start spending more time on your project. Really. Hey, I already got the lemonade mix. You can cross that off the list. My dad helped me buy it as a donation to the cause."

"That's really nice," Alex said sincerely. "Tell him thanks."

"And don't worry," Ray said. "Your cleanup project is going to be the best. I promise."

Alex hoped so. But she was still worried about Kelly's billboard. Ray had heard that her group was working on it in a secret location.

Would it be good enough to beat Alex's cleanup campaign?

CHAPTER 8

On Wednesday after school Alex went back to Talkin'
Tees.

Roger looked up in delight as she hurried into
the shop. He was wearing a T-shirt that said THIS
SPACE FOR RENT.

"Alex Mack, my favorite environmentalist! Where
do you get these outrageous hats? Maybe we should
go into business together and sell them here."

Alex grinned. Today she was wearing a black felt
hat with a silk rose on the brim. It was an old hat—
maybe you could even call it an antique. She'd
bought it at a yard sale from an elderly lady and
promised her she would always take good care of it.

All Alex's hats were really special to her. But
sometimes Annie teased her about them. It felt cool
to have somebody compliment them for a change.

"Thanks, Mr.—"

He stopped her with a mock scowl.

"I mean Roger."

"Much better," he said, breaking into a warm smile. But then he looked concerned. "Alex, I hope you're not here for your T-shirts yet. Like I said, it'll probably be Friday before I have them ready."

"Oh, I know," Alex said. "That's not why I'm here. I brought you something." She opened up her backpack and pulled out a leather pouch of cash. She counted out ones, fives, and tens. It was almost two hundred dollars. "Here."

Roger stared at the cash. "What's this?"

"It's a deposit. I know it's nowhere near the whole amount, but I hope it will be all right."

"But, Alex, we made a deal, remember? You don't have to give me a deposit."

Alex left the money on the counter. "I know we did. But this is the first time I ever did anything like this. The shirts are really selling well. The kids at school love the design you helped us come up with. So I felt like . . . I don't know, like I wanted to do things the right way, the way any other customer would. Besides, it makes me nervous having so much cash around."

Roger hesitated, but then he took the money and bowed slightly. "I accept your offer in the spirit in which it is offered. So, how's your project coming?"

"It's going great!" Alex exclaimed. "I mean, it's a lot of work, but I can't wait till Saturday. It's going to be fun."

"Wish I could be there. But I'm closing early on Friday. My wife, Gloria, and I are going to Seattle this weekend for this huge outdoor concert. You wouldn't believe how many T-shirts we can sell at those things. Anyway, be sure and come to get your shirts by, say, three-thirty, before we close?"

"Great! See you then!" Alex turned to leave just as the bell over the door tinkled.

Kelly breezed right past Alex without saying hello. "Hi, Mr. Kapsalakis."

The shopkeeper winced. "Roger, please. 'Mr. Kapsalakis' makes me feel so old. To me 'Mr. Kapsalakis' will always be my old man."

"Whatever," Kelly muttered under her breath so only Alex could hear. Then she smiled sweetly. "Are my flyers ready?"

"You bet. Gloria finished them up last night while I was at me computer class. I'll get them." He stepped into the back room.

Alex headed for the door.

"Wait, Alex!" Kelly called to her. "Let me give you one of my flyers."

Alex waited out of curiosity as Kelly dug in her purse for her wallet. When Roger came back and put a box on the counter, she handed him a credit card.

While the shopkeeper rang up the sales, Kelly

opened the box and pulled out a glossy multicolored flyer. For a moment she just held it up and admired it, then she handed it to Alex. "Have one. Or maybe you'd like some extras to hand out and put up around town?"

Alex took the flyer and stared at it in disbelief. It must have cost a fortune to print, she thought. On it was a four-color photo of a rock band named Absolute Flak. They were just a local group, but they were getting pretty popular. Robyn had heard them and said they were great.

But then Alex read the words beneath the picture, and her heart sank:

Party for the environment!!!
Free concert with
Absolute Flak!!!
See the unveiling of
the Danielle Atron Junior High School
Pick Up Paradise Billboard
This Saturday, 10:00 A.M. until . . . ?
Great food will be available for sale
All profits go to pay for the billboard
Come party for a good cause!

Alex closed her eyes. It could *not* say Saturday. It could *not!*

She opened her eyes.

It did.

The billboard was one thing. Alex thought that

her cleanup day could compete with that. But how could she compete with a band?

"How did you get a popular group like this to play for a tiny school project?" Alex asked.

Kelly shrugged. "The drummer's my second cousin. So, do you want to put up some posters for me, Alex? Let's see, you could put some up at the Laundromat, the post office—wherever it is that you eighth graders hang out."

"Uh, I don't think so, Kelly. See you." Alex shoved open the shop door.

"Hope to see you at the concert!" Kelly called after her. Then her hand flew to her mouth. "Oops! I guess you'll be doing your little cleanup thing then, won't you? Too bad." But she didn't sound sorry at all.

Alex hurried down the street to get as far away from Talkin' Tees as she could. She felt like bursting into tears, but no way was she going to let Kelly see her cry.

Alex had put so much work into her project. And now Kelly had totally trashed it, just because she was lucky enough to be distantly related to a drummer.

It's not fair! Alex thought. *There's no way in the world I can possibly compete with live music by a cool group at a free outdoor concert.*

Face it, Alex, you're done for, she told herself. Who wanted to spend the day picking up trash in the hot sun when they could be partying at the coolest Save the Earth concert of the year?

CHAPTER 9

On Friday Alex came home from school and dumped her books and jacket on her desk. Then she lay back on her bed, with her eyes closed and her headphones on, thinking about tomorrow. She and Robyn and Nicole had done all they could to publicize their event. They'd sold tons of shirts. They'd put up posters everywhere. They'd gotten businesses to donate work gloves, and they'd had plenty of money for trash bags.

Ray had helped some, too. But he'd been so busy working on Louis's project—and doing extra math homework and chores and playing the horn—that she'd hardly seen him at all.

By tomorrow night her sister Annie would either be saying, "Hey, Alex, you really pulled off a fabulous event. I'm proud of you." Or "Hey, Alex, you really bombed."

"Hey, Alex . . ."

"Hey, *Alex!*"

Alex jumped as Annie pulled one earphone away from her head and hollered, "Can you hear me?"

"Ow! Yeah. Stop shouting," Alex said. She pulled her headphones off and rubbed her ear.

Annie stood with her hands on her hips. "Did you get the messages?"

"What messages?"

Annie snorted impatiently. "The ones I left on your desk."

Alex hopped up and went to her desk. She shoved her books aside and picked up her jacket. There lay a piece of paper with Annie's handwriting on it. "Is this it? I didn't see it when I came in."

"The messages were on the answering machine when I got home."

Alex quickly read Annie's neat, perfect handwriting: "Call Nicole as soon as you get home. She says its *urgent!*" There was a line and then another message: "Ditto Robyn. Ditto *urgent!*"

Trembling, Alex hurried to the phone and quickly tapped in Nicole's home phone number. Her friend answered on the fourth ring.

"Nicole! It's Alex! What's wrong?"

"Bad news, Alex. But not too bad," Nicole added

quickly. "My relatives are throwing a surprise birth-day party for my great-grandmother tonight. She turned one hundred today. Mom swears she told me it was tonight, but I thought it was next week. And Mom's making me go."

"Wow," Alex said. "Tell your great-grandmother happy birthday for me."

"You don't understand," Nicole went on. "She lives three hours away. We're leaving in like two minutes! So I can't get to the cleanup tomorrow until late."

"Oh, no!" Alex said.

"I know, I know. I'd get up and leave at three A.M. to get back here if it were up to me. You know my mom, though. She is not a morning person. But I'll be there eventually—I promise!"

Alex took a breath and calmed down. It was not that big a deal. She and Robyn would manage the setup. And Ray, too—maybe. There would be plenty of other people showing up, too. "We'll be fine," Alex assured her. "Don't worry. Have a good time with your great-grandmother. Just come when you can. I'm sure there'll be lots of trash waiting for you when you get there."

"Wouldn't miss it!" Nicole insisted. "Mom's honking. Gotta go. I'll see you tomorrow!"

Alex hung up and then dialed Robyn's number. Thank goodness for Robyn, Alex thought. Sure, she grumbled a lot, but she was loyal and dependable. You could always count on her when you needed her.

The phone rang several times. At last someone picked up. But no one said hello.

"Hello? Is somebody there?" Alex asked.

"Al-exxx!" she heard somebody gasp.

Was this some kind of joke? A prank phone call? But wait—Alex was the one making the call.

"Who is this?" Alex demanded in her best assertive voice.

"Al-exxx, it's me," the voice whispered. "Robyn."

"Robyn—what's wrong? Are you okay?"

"Virus ... Cough, cough. Got laryngitis. Can hardly ... talk. Fever. Had to go home from school early. Mom won't let me out of the—cough—housssse."

Oh, no. Robyn had caught the virus the school nurse had warned the students about in the assembly! "Robyn, I'm so sorry," Alex said. "Are you feeling okay? Can I do anything for you? Do you want me to—"

"Teee-shirrrts," Robyn hissed.

"T-shirts?" Alex repeated, puzzled. "Oh, the T-shirts!" Alex cried out when she realized what Robyn had been trying to say. Robyn had volunteered to pick them up. Alex glanced at her watch.

It was 3:25. Roger was going to close up any minute and leave!

"Robyn! Didn't you get them?" Alex shouted frantically. "We were supposed to pick up the shirts by three-thirty. Roger's closing early!"

"You . . . didn't tell me."

"But I—" Alex stopped. Robyn hadn't been with her on Wednesday when Roger told her he was closing early. "I—I guess I forgot to tell you."

"Cough, cough," was all Robyn had to say.

Alex decided she'd have to give it her best try. Shifting into high gear, she said, "Robyn! I gotta go—now. Bye!"

She slammed down the phone, picked it right back up, and quickly dialed Roger's number.

The line was busy!

"No time to wait," Alex said to herself as she grabbed her hat and ran down the stairs.

"Alex!" Annie said as her sister raced past. "What in the world—?"

"Gotta get the T-shirts!" Alex said over her shoulder. "They're going to close in five minutes."

"Wait!" Annie shouted. "How are you getting there? How do you plan to carry all those boxes?"

"I don't know, Annie. I've just got to get there."

Annie grabbed the house key. "Let me run upstairs and get some money, Alex. Then we can bike over—that'll be the fastest way. And I'll pay for a cab to get the boxes home."

Alex stared in amazement as her sister ran upstairs. Annie really *was* smart, even under pressure. And never before had Alex appreciated her brains as much as she did today.

Seconds later the two sisters were biking as fast as they could toward Talkin' Tees. But as soon as the shop came into view, Alex's heart sank. A bright red Closed sign hung on the inside of the door.

"Oh, no!" Alex wailed. She dropped her bike to the sidewalk, ran up to the door, and pulled in vain on the handle.

First Kelly and her amazing rock concert. Now this.

The T-shirts she had to have by tomorrow were locked up till Monday morning!

CHAPTER 10

Alex peered through the glass. She pounded on the door with her fist. Maybe Roger and Gloria hadn't actually left yet.

"Roger!" she called out. She waited. She pounded. She called again. But no one came. The shop was silent, the lights all turned off.

"Look, Alex," Annie said, pointing to the door. "There's a note."

An envelope labeled "Alex Mack" was taped to the glass right above her head. Alex yanked it down and ripped it open. Inside was a note written in hasty handwriting.

Dear Alex,
 Sorry, but we have to split or we'll never

make it. Our old VW van is not very fast. But don't worry. Sky has a key. He's staying at his grandmother's this weekend. The number is 555-2564. Call him and he'll help you out.

Have a great Saturday!

Roger & Gloria

P.S.: Don't worry about paying till next week. I'm cool.

Alex spotted a pay phone on the corner and dug into her pockets as she ran toward it. She dropped in change, then quickly dialed the number.

"Hello?" an elderly lady said.

Alex asked for David.

"Sky?" the woman said in a thick foreign accent that Alex didn't recognize. "Not here. He goes to the movies with his friends. Do you wish me to have him telephone you?"

"No, thanks," Alex said, feeling a pang of disappointment. "I'll try him again later."

"Maybe eleven or twelve o'clock, yes?"

"Okay, bye," Alex said.

She hung up and walked back to the shop. "No luck," she said to Annie without even looking at her as she went by. When Alex reached the storefront, she cupped her hands against the glass and peered inside. She could see several boxes sitting right on the front counter. Each had the name Mack written on it in big black marker. She just had to get those T-shirts!

"Annie. Cover for me."

"What?" Annie said.

"I've got to get the shirts! And there's only one way I can see to do it." She stepped back and squinted in concentration.

"Alex, no! Alex, you can't—"

But Alex had made up her mind. Ignoring her sister's protests, she looked around to see if anyone was watching, then dissolved into a silvery puddle.

While Annie stood by, nervously looking in all directions, Alex seeped under the door and into the shop. Then she slithered across the floor and behind the counter. Seconds later she'd re-formed into her normal body.

Alex felt a little funny about being in the shop after hours. There was no way she'd ever break into a store as her regular self. But this wasn't exactly breaking in, she told herself. Her morphed form hadn't actually broken anything to get inside. And anyway, Roger had given her permission to go into the shop and take her T-shirts. He'd even left a key with his son. She'd just used a different "key" to get in!

Alex quickly opened a box. Yes—these were hers. The shirts looked great. But there was no time for checking them out now. She grabbed one box and headed for the door. First she looked to see if there was a security alarm system, but there wasn't, so Alex turned the lock and stepped outside.

"Hold the door, Annie," she whispered "I've got to get the other boxes."

Annie hurried over, looking around nervously. "Hurry, Alex!" she urged.

Alex quickly brought the other boxes outside and let the door close behind her. Yanking on the handle, she made sure the door had locked securely. She didn't want anybody else going in while the shop was closed.

"Uh, Alex?" she heard Annie say in a tense voice.

Alex turned around and found herself staring into Kelly's face. She was carrying a plastic shopping bag from the drugstore on the corner.

"What have you got there, Alex?" Kelly said in her super-sweet voice.

Alex gulped. "Um, T-shirts."

Kelly glanced from the box to the shop—with the red Closed sign swaying slightly behind the glass. "The shop's closed," Kelly observed. "How'd you get the shirts—walk through walls?"

Alex opened her mouth—and choked. Not a word would come out.

"Of course not!" Annie snapped briskly. "Mr. Kapsalakis made arrangements for Alex to get a key."

Alex grinned. That was the truth, after all. Hooray

for Annie and her quick thinking! Then she watched in amazement as Annie opened a box and held up a T-shirt in front of Kelly's face.

"Lovely shade of blue," Annie said in a cheery voice. "An extra-large, by the looks of it. Want to buy one? It's for a good cause."

Kelly smiled politely at the shirt. "Thanks," she said flatly. "I'll be sure to wear it at my concert on Saturday. But I need a small. Can I pay you later, Alex?"

"No," Annie said bluntly before Alex could think of what to say.

Kelly glared at Annie, then handed Alex some money. "Now, Alex," Kelly said with a big smile. "Don't you forget to come join us if you feel like partying and listening to some rock and roll. Or maybe you'd rather pick up trash all day. Whatever . . ." Kelly turned on her chunky heels and walked off.

Alex stared in admiration at her sister when Kelly was gone. She didn't even care if Kelly had been her usual rude self. She was just so totally glad she'd had her sister around to help her out.

"Thanks a whole lot, Annie. You really told her!"

"No problem," Annie said with a grin. "That's what big sisters are for."

Annie then went to the pay phone and called for a cab. While they waited, Annie couldn't resist giving Alex a little lecture.

"You know, Alex. You really shouldn't have broken in to Mr. Kapsalakis's store. It's a terrible misuse of your powers."

"But he said I could go in!" Alex argued. "And he left me a key. What's the difference?"

"I'm not sure," Annie admitted, "but I feel weird about it. Just promise me you won't do it again. Okay?"

"Okay," Alex promised. She sincerely hoped she'd never have to do anything like it ever again, too.

"And what are you going to tell Mr. Kapsalakis about how you got the shirts—without the key? He's bound to ask his son about it."

"You're the smart one in the family," Alex said with a grin. "I'm sure you'll think of something!"

The cab arrived and they packed all the boxes into the trunk. Annie and Alex biked back home and met the cabdriver there. Soon the boxes were stacked neatly on the walk in front of the house.

Annie fished in her pockets, then turned to Alex. "Have you got a house key?"

"No," Alex said. "I thought you had it."

Annie bit her lip. "Well, I did have it. But I guess I put it on my desk when I ran up to get my money before we left. How stupid of me."

Alex peered closely at her big sister. Something weird was happening to her. Was she . . . ? Could she possibly be . . . ?

Annie was blushing! She was as red as a tomato.

"What are you staring at?" Annie snapped.

"I can't remember ever seeing you blush before!" Alex crowed. "Miss Perfect is blushing."

Annie glared at Alex. "Don't call me that!"

"Well, don't get mad, Annie," Alex said, trying to control her laughter. "It's just that you're always so good at everything. You're always so neat and orderly and perfect. You never make mistakes."

"Is that what you think?" Annie sat down on the front steps. She looked up at her sister with a half smile. "There are a lot of things I'm not good at."

"Like what?" Alex challenged as she sat down beside her.

"Like making friends—the way you do. You've got three best friends. But I don't. And believe me, I do make mistakes. Lots of them. All the time."

"Yeah, right," Alex said with a laugh.

"I *do*," Annie insisted. "That's what scientific research is all about, Alex. Trying things, failing, making mistakes, then trying something different. You keep at it until something works. Mistakes often tell me something new about my experiment, or they give me information I never knew."

"Really?" Alex was amazed. This was a totally new idea for her. She stared at her sister thoughtfully.

"Yeah, really. I never get it right the first time. I guess that's why they call it an experiment."

"It's gone now," Alex said finally.

"What?"

"Your red face."

That made Annie blush all over again.

"So what do we do now?" Alex asked. "Sit out here till Mom and Dad get home?"

Annie made a face. "They won't be home for a couple of hours, and I've got homework to do."

On a Friday night? Alex thought. "I know a way to get in," she suggested.

"No, Alex!" Annie cried. "No morphing. Don't you dare."

"But, Annie, it's so easy. Why not?"

"Because—"

The phone began to ring inside the house. The sun was getting hot. Annie threw up her hands. "Oh, I give up. Do it. Ohhh! I can't believe it—twice in one afternoon. But hurry. And don't blame me if you get stuck!"

"Be nice," Alex said just before she morphed into a puddle. Then she added in a gurgling voice, "Or I won't let you in!" In a flash she scooted under the door.

Once inside, Alex quickly changed back to normal.

Annie was pounding on the door. "Alex! Don't you dare lock me out!"

Alex grinned. It sure was fun to tease her big sister. Of course she'd let her in.

As soon as she got the phone. . . .

CHAPTER 11

On Saturday Alex was up early, as nervous as if she were about to go onstage. A lot of kids had put down money for their T-shirts from her group during the past week. But how many people would show up to get their shirts and help with the Pick Up Paradise cleanup?

Alex's mom dashed off to meet with Danielle Atron, who was going to be observing the day's events. Her dad had to go to work early, but he'd offered to drive her and all her stuff over to the cleanup site. Annie had to go to the library, but promised to come by later and see how Alex was doing.

Alex loaded up her dad's car with trash bags, gloves, sunscreen, the boxes of T-shirts, a card table, and a couple of folding chairs. Then she waited anxiously in the living room while her dad went upstairs to collect some paperwork to take to his office.

Alex jumped when the doorbell rang. *Maybe Nicole got back earlier than expected*, she hoped as she dashed for the door. *Or maybe Robyn got better overnight!*

Alex yanked open the door.

Ray stood on the front porch. He wiggled his two hands in the air. "Could you use a couple of these?"

Alex had never been so happy to see Ray's cheery face. "How'd you guess?" she said with a big smile.

"ESP?" Ray picked up two huge thermos jugs and stepped inside. "I brought the lemonade," he said, "as promised." Then he sank sideways onto a big stuffed chair in the living room, his legs dangling over the arm. "Actually," he said, "Nicole called me and told me that she was was going to be out of town and that Robyn was sick. I thought that even with all your"—he looked furtively around the room and whispered—"special powers, you might need a little help this morning."

Alex flopped down on the couch. "You're right. It's hard to believe, but sometimes even morphing and zapping things can't fix them."

"I'll take your word for it," Ray said.

Alex plucked at the fringe of an afghan hanging over the back of the couch. "I thought you were supposed to do something with Louis this morning."

"I was," Ray said. "But Louis's goat thing is pretty simple. He's got everything under control. I figured you needed me more, with Robyn and Nicole out of business."

Alex glowed briefly, blushing. "Thanks, Ray."

Mr. Mack came running down the stairs then. "Ready to go, Alex? Hi, Ray. Come on, guys," he said without stopping. Alex knew he was in too much of a rush to see her glowing complexion.

Soon they were driving toward the meadow. The weather was gorgeous. *Yes,* Alex thought as they pulled up in front of the field, *conditions are perfect for a prize-winning project! And this spot definitely needs cleaning up,* Alex thought as she jumped out of the car. Her excitement was growing as she and Ray took out their supplies. They set things up on a card table in the shade of a huge tree where they'd be easy to find.

"Now, what time do you need me to pick you up?" Mr. Mack asked.

"I'll call you, Dad," Alex said. "Thanks for the ride over."

"Good luck," he said, then drove off toward Paradise Valley Chemical.

Alex and Ray sat down and waited.

And waited.

Alex checked her watch and rearranged some work gloves and T-shirts on the table. The kids should be arriving soon.

Ray wiped his forehead on his sleeve and got up to pour himself a cup of lemonade from the thermos jug. "Man, it's getting hot already," he said. "And we haven't even started."

He sat back down beside Alex and waited some more. "Want some lemonade?" he asked her after ten minutes.

Alex shook her head. She looked down the road to see if any cars were coming.

Ray slurped the last of his lemonade, then tossed the cup over his shoulder.

"Ray!"

"Just kidding, Alex." He stood up and grabbed a pair of gloves. "Time to go to work, I guess." He pulled on the gloves, picked up his cup, and stuffed it into a trash bag. "How am I doin'?" he asked with a grin.

Alex couldn't help but smile.

"Come on," he said, pulling Alex up from her seat. "Let's get started. The other kids will show up any minute now. I promise."

Alex halfheartedly picked up a soda can and dunked it into the trash bag Ray held open. She was starting to worry. Things were way too quiet.

"Maybe everybody slept late," Ray suggested. "After all, it is Saturday."

"Maybe."

After they'd picked up litter for about twenty minutes, Alex heard a car coming. She shaded her eyes against the sun and looked down the road.

A stretch limo pulled to a stop with a van and another car not far behind. The limo driver came around and opened the door. Danielle Atron stepped out, followed by Alex's mom.

A couple of reporters and photographers jumped out of the other vehicles and followed Danielle as she walked up to Alex's table.

With her face frozen into a smile, Danielle whispered to Alex, "Where are all the kids? I promised these reporters a photo opportunity. Your mother told me there'd be a wonderful project going on here right now. But there's nothing happening here. I don't see even one photo op!"

"Hey," Ray called to the photographers. He grabbed a trash bag and started stuffing it with litter, his eyes never leaving the cameras. "You can take a picture of me. Come on, Alex! Let's show these dudes how to clean up."

Alex glanced at her mother and cringed. Looking embarrassed, Barbara Mack was trying to come up with some sort of explanation.

And it's all my fault, Alex thought. But she felt worse for her mother than she did for herself.

Uh-oh! Alex felt her face starting to grow warmer. She was glowing again!

Ray suddenly grabbed her and pulled her toward the field so her face was turned away from the adults. "Alex, look at this!" he babbled. Then he whispered under his breath, "Think of all the teachers at school sitting on the stage in their underwear."

Alex snorted as she stifled a giggle. It was a silly thought, but it helped distract her from her own embarrassment, and she felt her golden glow begin to fade. "Thanks, Ray," she whispered.

Then Alex took three deep breaths and did the only two things she could think of.

She told a little white lie to cover for her mom.

And she helped out her competition.

She forced a bright smile and announced, "Um, actually, the cleanup had to be rescheduled for later today. Right now the real happening event is over at the park. Kelly is going to unveil her billboard, and she's got a group called Absolute Flak doing an outdoor concert. You don't want to miss that!"

Danielle sighed in relief. "Excellent! This way," she called out to the reporters. She strode back to her limo and slipped inside as the reporters scampered back to their cars.

Mrs. Mack gave Alex a quick hug. "I guess I'll see you a little later, then, huh?" Then she hurried to catch up with Danielle.

Alex watched as the cars screeched off toward the park, which was just over the next hill, about three-quarters of a mile away. Then she kicked the nearest aluminum can as hard as she could and sent it sailing across the field.

This was absolutely the worst day of her entire life!

CHAPTER 12

"Come on, Al," Ray said. "Don't kick the poor defenseless litter. Besides, you'll just have to go over and pick it up anyway."

Alex stomped over to the shade and leaned against the tree. "Face it, Ray. Nobody's coming," she said, staring at the ground.

"But—" Ray stopped as they heard the faint sounds coming from the direction of the park. An electric guitar was tuning up. First they heard some chords, then some screeching feedback.

A few seconds later, and *whomp!*

The opening chords of a rock song floated over the hill.

"Man, they must have the amplifiers turned up full blast!" Ray exclaimed. He cupped his ear, straining to hear what song they were playing.

Alex felt totally rotten. Everybody from school was probably over at the park having a good time, not standing around in a field full of stinky litter. Even Ray wished he were over there, she could tell.

With a long, frustrated sigh, Alex plopped down to the base of the tree. "Ray, this is silly," she said. "Why don't you go on over there—"

"No way!" Ray insisted. "I'm staying here with you. We've got a cleanup job to do."

Alex just shook her head. "No, Ray. Two people? It would take us a week to clean this whole place up."

"But—"

"Forget it, Ray." Alex got up and began stuffing the work gloves back into the box. "I'm the chairperson of this project, and I am making an executive decision to shut it down, right now."

"But, Alex, you can't!"

Alex shoved him toward the park. "I just did! Now go have a great time at the park. This project is canceled."

Ray put his hand on her shoulder. "What are you going to do?"

"I don't know," Alex said. Then she tried to smile. "Maybe we can try again for next Saturday. The contest will be over, but we can still do the cleanup. Kelly won't be around to interfere."

"Well, if you're sure . . ." Ray said.

Alex nodded firmly.

"I have been dying to see this band," Ray admitted. He grabbed her hand. "Come on, let's go. It'll be a blast."

But Alex wouldn't budge. "You go on. I'll be over there later."

"But, Alex—"

"Ray, I really just want to be by myself for a little while. Okay?"

Ray looked into her eyes to make sure she was serious. "Okay. But can I buy a T-shirt, at least?"

Alex tossed him a large purple one. "It's on the house."

"Gee, thanks!" Ray exclaimed. He pulled it on over his other T-shirt, then waved and jogged off toward the park. "I'll save you a seat!" he called back over his shoulder.

Alex watched him go, then sat down at the card table and buried her head in her arms. She felt horrible. Miserable. Awful. Yucky. Totally bummed.

No way am I going to that concert, she thought stubbornly. *Maybe I'll just stay here till I biodegrade so I'll never have to show my face at school again.*

She sat there awhile longer, feeling sorry for herself. A slight breeze ruffled her hair. Across the field a couple of birds warbled an intricate song. She wondered briefly what kind of birds they were.

Still and quiet now, she listened to bees buzzing. Propping her head in her hand, she watched a black and orange monarch butterfly land on a yellow wildflower she couldn't name.

Alex was glad she lived here in Paradise Valley and not someplace where everything was cement or asphalt. It was beautiful in the meadow, feeling the sun on her face and hearing the wind through the trees.

Except the litter is gross, Alex thought. The litter really ruined it all.

She stood up and quietly slipped on her work gloves. She snagged two black trash bags and bent down to pick up a gum wrapper, a soda can, another soda can. Ewww! A sock!

She sorted things as she went: recyclables in one bag, trash in the other.

A department store bag. Another soda can. A wadded-up candy wrapper.

This is my town, Alex thought. *My Paradise Valley. And I don't want it messed up like this anymore.*

A hawk soared overhead, and Alex stopped to watch it.

Awesome.

With a renewed sense of purpose, she went back to her task, working quietly, steadily, an army of one, cleaning up a tiny patch of the incredibly huge planet earth. Her trash bag was soon half full. Would it make a difference? Alex believed it would.

When she reached the crest of the hill, she looked down toward the park.

And gasped!

CHAPTER 13

Alex couldn't believe it. From the edge of the park, she could see cars parked all over the grass. Hordes of kids were sprawled across the lawn in front of a stage where Absolute Flak was playing really good—and really loud—rock. The kids were sitting on their blankets on the ground or dancing on the grass; some were playing Frisbee, and others were walking to or from the vendors' stands.

This party was a really big deal. But that wasn't the shocker.

What Alex couldn't believe was the litter.

The park trash cans were already overflowing. Snack wrappers and other paper lay scattered all over the grounds.

A crumpled piece of paper blew up against her

leg. She grabbed it and unfolded it. It was one of Kelly's glossy flyers advertising the Pick Up Paradise concert.

Kelly's project to increase awareness of the litter problem was actually creating more litter itself!

Alex watched as the band took a break and Kelly walked up to the microphone.

"And now," Kelly announced, "the moment you've all been waiting for!" She pointed toward the baseball field at a billboard that was covered by a huge canvas sheet.

"I'd like to present to you the new student-designed, student-created Pick Up Paradise billboard!"

A couple of kids yanked on the covering till it fell.

"Cool!" Alex heard someone shout out. The crowd started clapping.

The billboard was handmade. You could tell it had been created and painted by students and not by a professional billboard company, and yet that only added to its charm. A huge figure of a teenage girl—that was painted to look a lot like Kelly—towered over the crowd. There was a soda can in her hand, and her arm was raised over a drawing of a trash barrel, as if she were about to drop the can in.

Big hot-pink letters proclaimed PICK UP PARADISE— FOR THE CHILDREN. The letters were covered with lightbulbs.

"Watch this," Kelly told the crowd. "It lights up. And it moves." Then she shouted, "Flip the switch!"

Suddenly Alex had an overwhelming desire to do something really awful. With a single flick of her fingertips, she could zap the billboard and ruin it. It would be so simple. She could ruin it as badly as her cleanup day was ruined.

She started to zap it.

But then she changed her mind.

Kelly had beaten her fair and square. It would be a cheap shot to destroy her billboard. Alex didn't want to play that way.

So she did nothing but watch as somebody flipped a switch on a generator and the billboard came to life. The arm shot up and down with a jerky motion, as if it was tossing the aluminum can but never letting go.

Lights flashed like a Las Vegas nightclub.

Rock music blared from hidden speakers.

Suddenly the swinging arm swung around and ripped completely off. Kids scattered as the arm crashed to the ground, still clutching the aluminum can.

Alex tried hard not to laugh, but she couldn't help it. She couldn't have done better if she'd tried to mess it up on purpose with her out-of-the-ordinary powers.

"Turn it off! Turn it off!" Kelly was screaming as the audience hooted with laughter.

Beep! Beep!

"Alex! What is going on?"

Alex turned around to see her dad drive up with Annie hanging out the window.

"We came by to check up on you and saw all your stuff just sitting out there in the middle of nowhere!" Annie said as she got out of the car. "What happened to your project? Did you—"

Suddenly Annie stopped, with her mouth hanging open, and stared at Kelly's billboard. She covered her mouth and burst out laughing. Then she stopped laughing. "Alex," she whispered, "is that you? Are you making this happen?"

"It's not me, Annie. I swear. Kelly's doing it all by herself."

Their dad walked up beside them then, but he didn't even seem to notice the flashing busted billboard. "Hi, Alex. We brought you the T-shirts you left over in the field. What would you like us to do with them?"

Alex thought for a moment. The band was taking a break, and Kelly's billboard was out of order. Maybe she could slip up onstage and make an announcement for the kids to pick up their shirts. She had extras to sell, too, and this might be a good time and place to unload them.

"Annie, quick. Help me carry some shirts on-stage," Alex said decisively.

George and Annie helped Alex lug the boxes to the stage. Alex walked up to two of the guys in the band and asked if she could make an announcement. The drummer said sure. He walked over and adjusted the mike so it was the right height for Alex.

"Hey, listen up!" he shouted. "We have a girl here with an important announcement."

Alex's heart was beating like crazy as she stepped up to the mike.

"Um, hi. I'm Alex Mack." Her soft voice was instantly magnified and seemed to bounce loudly across the park. "And, um, I've got an announcement to make."

Alex took a breath and said, "First of all, a lot of you ordered T-shirts from my group this week." She held up a shirt. "Well, I have them here today. And you can pick them up in a minute.

"Second of all . . ."

She stared out into the sea of faces. Everyone seemed to be in a good mood, having a great time. Maybe she shouldn't say what was on her mind. It would just bring everybody down and ruin the concert.

A crumpled flyer blew across the grass right in front of the stage. She spotted a trash can near the food vendors that was overflowing with garbage.

"Second of all," she blurted out, "today is supposed to be about cleaning up Paradise Valley, not messing it up. But look around you. This concert is creating litter. Some of it is even blowing into that field over there where—where I'm doing my cleanup project today. Even the flyers about this Pick Up Paradise concert—which is supposed to be about cleaning up this town—are all over the ground."

The crowd was nearly silent now, staring at her. Alex was surprised she wasn't blushing—or worse yet glowing! Maybe it was because she wasn't embarrassed about what she was saying.

"I think the litter problem in Paradise Valley is not just some anonymous person tossing fast-food wrappers out their car window as they zoom through town. It happens every time one of us drops something on the ground and thinks that doing it just once doesn't matter.

"So on behalf of all the people who live here, I'd like to ask you to take care of Paradise Valley and take care of your litter. And anybody who could spare a half hour or so today is welcome to come join me in my cleanup project."

Alex realized she'd twisted up the T-shirt she was holding, so she shook it out. "Um, thanks, everybody!"

At first the crowd was silent. Then she could hear

kids talking, but she couldn't tell what they were saying. Did they agree with her, or were they going to laugh her off the stage?

A guy from the band walked over to where Alex stood. It was the cute one, the one in the middle of the picture on Kelly's flyer.

"Hey, Alex," he said with a nice smile. "I'm Josh."

"Hi, Josh," Alex said shyly.

"You know, I like what you're saying. You've really got your head together about all this."

"Yeah, well, I guess," she said softly.

Josh shoved his longish dark hair back from his face and leaned into the mike. "Hellooooo, Paradise Valley!"

"Hellooooo!" the crowd roared back.

"How's everybody enjoying this beautiful day?" This time the crowd roared and clapped and cheered.

Josh draped his arm across Alex's shoulders and pulled her toward the mike. "You know, my friend Alex here is really laying it on the line. One of the reasons we took this gig is because we're big on the environment. It's a good cause that we like to promote whenever we can."

The drummer pounded on his drums and cymbal as the crowd cheered again.

Josh raised his hand for silence. The crowd settled

down. "But you know, Alex is right. It's great to buy a T-shirt with an impressive slogan on it. And it's great to party for a good cause. But we gotta do more than that. Because it's not just about a slogan or a party. It's about saving the planet, our mother ship. Like Alex says, we ought to be working for the cause first, man. Then we party. What do you say we all join Alex and Pick Up Paradise? I mean till there's not a scrap of litter in sight. Then, if it's okay with the sponsors for this thing, we'll come back here, and me and the guys will party till the cows come home. How does that sound, Alex?"

Alex was nearly jumping up and down. "That sounds great!"

"Are you with us?" Josh shouted into the microphone.

"YESSS!" the crowd shouted.

"Hey," he asked Alex, "you got any T-shirts in my size?"

"Sure!" Alex held one out, and he paid her for it on the spot.

Josh pulled it on over his tank top. "One more thing," he said into the mike. "The band and I will personally autograph the T-shirt of anybody who helps out with Alex's cleanup today. All right?"

"All right!" the crowd cheered in response.

"Okay, Alex," Josh said, "lead the way. We're right behind you."

Another member of the band came up and spoke into the mike, explaining that several of the food vendors had set trash cans aside that were marked for recyclables.

Alex remembered something else she needed to say and stepped up to the mike. "We've also got lots of work gloves. Please wear them when you're picking up trash so nobody gets hurt. And if you turn them in when you're done, we can wash them and use them again."

"All right!" Josh shouted. "Let's do it! I'll see you all back here in a couple of hours."

Ray and Louis ran up onstage. Nicole had finally arrived, too, and had heard it all.

"Alex, you were great!" Ray exclaimed. "I am really proud of you. Really!"

"What'd I tell you?" Nicole said. "It's a new Alex—taking charge!"

Ray shook his head. "Not new, just the same Alex I've always known."

Alex gave Ray a hug.

"Definitely excellent!" Louis added. "Hey, can we help you out here?" he said as they were mobbed by concertgoers who wanted T-shirts.

"Thanks, guys." Alex said. She and her friends handed out T-shirts, and also work gloves and garbage bags.

A lot of kids had nice things to say to Alex when they picked up their shirts and supplies.

When Scott came up to her to get gloves and a bag, he said, "You really made us think, Alex. That was a great speech."

But Kelly was right behind him, grabbing his arm. "Scott, come on," she said with a flirty pout. "You promised you'd help me get the billboard fixed."

"Don't worry, Alex," he called as Kelly dragged him away. "I'll join you guys as soon as I can!"

Alex and her friends laughed.

"Got any adult large in flamingo pink left?" a familiar voice asked.

Alex whirled around. "Mom!"

With a big smile, Barbara Mack forked over the cash. "I'll take two, but better make Dad's extra large."

Alex handed over the shirts. Then she noticed her mom had a funny look on her face and had gotten a little watery around the eyes. "Alex, what you said up there—well, it was just beautiful," Mrs. Mack said. "And you're beautiful, too!" She gave Alex a hug.

Just then Danielle Atron shoved her way to the front of the crowd. She touched her hair and smiled at the reporters who'd followed her. "Yes, Alex, dear," Mrs. Atron said. "That was just lovely." She placed a hand on Alex's shoulder and said out of the corner of her mouth, "Smile for the cameras, dear."

The reporters were getting it all, and Danielle was loving it. She grabbed some work gloves from Louis and put them on and then led the reporters out across the park, pretending to pick up litter as they interviewed her.

Alex smiled as she surveyed the crowd fanning out across the park and the field beyond. She couldn't believe how many people were pitching in to help pick up trash. And she was surprised that the party mood remained. Some kids were even singing Absolute Flak songs as they worked. It was outrageous!

Tapping Alex on the shoulder, Louis cleared his throat. "Hey, Alex. I kind of owe you an apology. I guess it can be sort of fun to pick up other people's garbage, more fun than I thought."

"Thanks, Louis."

He shook his head as he wandered off with a black trash bag. Alex heard him say, "I just wish I'd brought a goat with me!"

Ray tapped Alex on the shoulder and held up a trash bag. "Want to share a bag with me?"

Alex grinned. "Sure, Ray. And thanks for all your help today."

"Hey—what are best friends for?"

With so many kids pitching in, the entire park

and the nearby meadow were spotless in just a few hours.

True to their word, Absolute Flak signed the T-shirt of anyone who helped out. The line for autographs was really long. Alex got one signed for Roger—as a thank-you for all he'd done—and one for Robyn, too.

"Hey, I didn't sign yours yet!" Josh said to Alex.

Alex turned around while he signed her shirt on the back.

"Okay, guys," Josh called to his band. "Ready to rock?"

The musicians hurried onto the stage and began tuning up. Alex, Louis, and Ray stood near the stage, where they could get a good view of the music being played.

Nicole suddenly came up to Alex from behind and said, "Alex! You should see your shirt!"

"What? What's wrong?"

Nicole put her hands on her hips and shook her head. "Nothing! It says, 'To Alex Mack, a very special girl. Love, Josh/Absolute Flak.' And then he wrote the date."

"Really?" Alex squealed. And to herself she thought, *Me? Special?*

"Hang on to that shirt," Nicole said. "It'll be priceless when they're famous!"

Alex and her friends settled down on the grass

as the band resumed their concert. Not only was everyone having a wonderful time, Alex noted, they were also being very careful with their trash.

The music was awesome. Sometimes Alex and her friends sang along, and once or twice Ray dragged Alex up to dance. And as the sunset bathed the park in beautiful shades of pink, Alex could hardly believe that her cleanup catastrophe had actually turned into one of the best days—and nights—of her life.

CHAPTER 14

"Do you need any help with that, Ray?"

It was Monday morning, and Alex and Ray were walking to school. In addition to his backpack, Ray was loaded down with posters and a plastic trash bag full of something—Alex had no idea what.

"Nope. I'm fine. This is stuff Louis and I need for our project display," Ray said.

All the kids who'd had a project were supposed to set up a display of their work in the gym that morning.

"Hey, where's your display?" Ray asked Alex.

"Nicole's bringing it. Her mom's driving her to school with it. Nicole insisted on doing it to make up for having to miss part of the project."

When they reached Louis's house, he came dashing out the front door yelling, "Wait up! I'll be right there." He ran around to the backyard and returned minutes later leading a real live goat.

"Hey, Billy," Ray said, petting the goat on the head. "How ya doin'?"

Alex couldn't believe what she was seeing. "Where in the world did you get it?"

"My dad got it from this guy at the farmers' market," Louis explained. "It's just a loan. Come on, Billy!" he called to the goat. "We're going to be late!"

"You see, Alex," Ray said, "this is why I wasn't around much to help you out with your project. I was busy looking for garbage to feed Billy."

"Uh-huh," Alex said. She was beginning to notice a kind of foul odor that surrounded them as they continued to walk. "Ray . . . ?" Alex said, sniffing the air. "Is that what I think it is in the garbage bag you're carrying?"

"It's Billy's lunch," Ray said, heaving the bag to his other shoulder.

"You mean it's garbage, Ray, right? You're carrying a bag of stinky garbage to school." Alex took a couple of steps away from Ray, to put some distance between herself and the stench.

"Well, it was either this or the cafeteria food," Ray said.

The gym was already full by the time the three

of them—plus Billy—got to school. Louis and Ray ran off to tie up Billy in a corner. They spread newspapers around and then fed the goat some of the garbage they'd hauled with them.

Alex found Nicole on the other side of the gym. She had just started setting up their display, which included a poster with photos of the Pick Up Paradise project and a T-shirt. The photos showed the meadows surrounding the park after the cleanup project, with beautiful shots of flowers and trees under a blue sky.

The vice principal came into the gym carrying a big cardboard ballot box with a slot cut in the top. He waved his arms and shouted, "Attention! Attention, kids!"

When everyone was listening, he announced, "Ms. Danielle Atron called me yesterday with a suggestion. After much deliberation, we've decided that we should allow you students to vote for the best project."

"How democratic," Nicole said with a laugh. "And it gets Danielle off the hook!"

Alex's heart sank. "What do you think?" she asked Nicole as they checked over their display. "Do we have a chance of winning if the kids are voting? I mean, the concert was such a blast."

"Yeah, but the billboard was such a bomb!" Nicole said.

Nicole and Alex giggled. Then Alex sighed and said, "Oh, well. I hope we win. But I had a great time Saturday anyway. Didn't you?"

"Yeah," Nicole agreed. "The only thing missing was Robyn. How is she? Did you call her?"

"I went by her house yesterday," Alex said as they strolled around the gym looking at projects. "Her mom wouldn't let me come in. She didn't want me to catch it," she said. "So Robyn came to her bedroom window, and we talked. Or I should say I talked and she wrote on a big tablet. She said she's feeling better. But her mom says it'll probably be Thursday or Friday before she can come back to school."

Nicole and Alex continued circling the gym and saw all sorts of interesting projects. One girl had made a videotape of herself singing a song she'd written about saving the earth. And a boy had made a book, with drawings and captions, about the local plants and animals that were threatened by pollution.

"Really cool stuff," Alex said.

Suddenly Nicole grabbed her arm, stopping her, and pointed. Alex looked over and saw what Nicole was pointing to, and she covered her mouth before she laughed out loud.

Kelly's display had been set up right next to Ray and Louis's goat. And it looked as though the goat preferred to munch on Kelly's project rather than the garbage that the boys had provided. Billy was chewing on the corner of a cardboard poster while Kelly was tugging at the poster to get it out of the grip of the goat's jaw.

Ray and Louis approached just then and pulled the chomping goat away from Kelly's display. With her hands on her hips, Kelly then stormed off toward the vice principal.

"I can't believe that goat almost ate Kelly's project!" Nicole said when she'd finally stopped laughing.

"I guess we're not the only ones who thought it was trash," Alex replied.

The first bell rang and kids sprinted toward lockers and homeroom.

Alex and Nicole locked pinkies and pulled. "Good luck!" they said at the same time.

"And don't forget to vote!" Alex added.

On Tuesday Danielle Atron marched into Danielle Atron Junior High School for her second assembly in less than a month. But this time Alex noticed that the students greeted her with a lot more enthusiasm. Alex was sitting in the auditorium with Nicole on one side and Ray and Louis on the other. They all waved at Mrs. Mack, who was sitting onstage.

The vice principal introduced Danielle again, and

she stepped up to the lectern with her hands full of newspapers. "First of all," she said, smiling brightly, "I'd like to say that I'm just ecstatic over the work you children have done."

"Here we go again," Louis joked.

"Shhhh!"

"Quiet!"

"Hush!"

Louis blinked. "Sorry," he whispered and slumped down in his seat.

Danielle held up a newspaper. "The Pick Up Paradise campaign was on the front page of several local and regional newspapers yesterday. Look"— she pointed at the picture—"there I am, right there! This is such wonderful publicity for our community and for Paradise Valley Chemical. Thank you for all your time and hard work and wonderful ideas."

There was a loud round of applause.

Danielle nodded, bowing slightly. "And now, what you've all been waiting for! I take great pleasure in announcing the winning Pick Up Paradise projects."

A hush fell over the auditorium. Alex crossed her fingers. She'd never wanted anything so much in her life. She peeked down the row at Scott, who was sitting with some of his friends. Just then he glanced her way and grinned. "Good luck!" he mouthed.

"Thanks!" she whispered back.

Then she grabbed Nicole's hand on one side and Ray's on the other. This was it!

"Second prize goes to ..." Danielle squinted at her index cards. "Something here about ... goats? Goats Against Garbage?"

"Yes! Yes!" Ray and Louis jumped out of their seats and high-fived it in the aisle.

"Ray Alvarado and Louis Driscoll," Danielle called out.

Alex clapped like crazy as they ran up onstage.

Danielle pointed at the spot where she wanted them to stand.

"First prize goes to ..."

Alex squeezed her eyes shut and just about crushed Nicole's hand.

"Kelly Phillips and her group—my, there certainly are a lot of you! I don't think we have time to read *all* the names." Danielle laughed. "For your community-service billboard and outdoor fund-raising concert!"

"No!" Nicole gasped as Kelly jumped up and waltzed onto the stage. She stood beaming next to Ray and Louis.

Alex's heart sank. Kelly was the first prize winner. Of course. The students had voted for the best project. How could she ever have believed she had a chance against one of the most popular girls at school?

Alex slid down in her seat. Another failure. Another opportunity to disappoint her parents. She hoped her sister would be kind.

Alex glanced at the stage and saw that Ray was scowling. Then she saw her mom get up out of her seat and interrupt Danielle. She whispered something to her and pointed to the index cards.

Danielle frowned, said, "Oh," and then turned back to the microphone. "I beg your pardon. It seems I, um . . . misspoke." She laughed in a fake way and said, "I should have said second runner-up and first runner-up. You know, kind of like the Miss America pageant?"

The auditorium buzzed with whispered comments.

"What's she talking about?" Nicole whispered to Alex.

Danielle flipped a card. "That brings me to first place winner—or shall we call it the grand prize winner? The project that you students voted to be the best in the entire school. . . ."

Alex's heart was pounding.

"And the winners are . . . Alex Mack, Nicole Wilson, Robyn Russo, and Ray Alvarado for their Pick Up Paradise cleanup project!"

Nicole was shouting and yanking on Alex's arm. "Come on, come on! We've got to go up there."

Alex couldn't move at first. Then she stumbled down the aisle and up the steps and onto the stage. She stood shyly next to Ray, but Danielle came over and pulled her and Nicole up to the microphone.

Kelly smiled stiffly at Alex as she walked past.

"Congratulations, girls," Danielle said. "Do you have anything to say?"

Nicole shook her head and pushed Alex up to the mike. But all Alex could manage was a soft, "Thanks!"

Then Danielle said, "Let's give all of our winners a great big round of applause."

The audience clapped loud and long.

"Uh, Ms. Atron?" Ray asked when the applause died down. "What do we win?"

Danielle seemed flustered. "Oh, dear. How could I forget?"

She gave Ray, Louis, and Kelly a certificate. Kelly looked as if she were going to be sick when she received hers.

Then Ms. Atron handed small engraved plaques to Alex and Nicole and Ray. There was one for Robyn, too.

Alex couldn't believe it! She'd never won anything so nice before. It was even engraved with her name.

"Oh, and one more thing," Danielle added.

Ray and Louis looked up expectantly.

"All of you are invited to have lunch with me in the Paradise Valley Chemical boardroom on Thursday. And we'll have our picture taken for the Sunday newspaper."

Louis made a face, and some of the kids in the audience tittered.

Ray just rolled his eyes and whispered to Alex, "All I can say is, the food had better be good!"

Alex laughed and said, "Maybe you ought to bring along Billy the goat—just in case!"

CHAPTER 15

Alex stuck a pushpin in the wall and hung up her award right over the head of her bed.

She tilted her head. Hmm. The plaque looked a little crooked. Or was it the autographed Absolute Flak poster beside it that was off? Alex fiddled with the plaque, trying to make it hang perfectly straight.

Oh, who cares? she thought at last. The important thing was she had won. It was so cool to have a real award at last, just like the ones Annie had.

Her parents had been so excited. They'd promised to take Alex and her friends out to dinner to celebrate as soon as Robyn was better. Annie had been great, too. She'd told Alex she was really proud of her. It was the first time Alex could ever remember Annie saying anything like that.

But the funny thing was, she realized now that it wasn't the award itself that was so important.

The real prize was how she felt inside.

She had a glowing feeling. And for once it wasn't on her face!

Alex flopped back on her bed with her head at the foot and her workboots on her pillow. She stared at her name, etched on the plaque.

A lot of kids were saying hi to her now in the halls at school. But it wasn't because she'd won an award or had her name announced at an assembly.

They'd said they related to what she had to say at the concert. They were really interested in what she was doing. Lots of kids had talked to her about starting a recycling club at school. Even Scott had said he'd like to join! Alex had set up an organizational meeting for the following Thursday.

The next project Alex wanted to do was to build recycling bins to place near the school Dumpster. She planned to call a company about recycling used white paper, too.

She'd also read in one of her magazines about a school that had a Feed the Pigs program. Lunchroom leftovers went into a special bin that a farmer picked up for his pigs. So all the mystery meat and leftover Twinkies wouldn't just rot in a landfill for some scientist like Annie to dig up one day in the future. Alex and Nicole were going to see if they could find some farmers in their area who had hungry pigs.

Alex grabbed a spiral notebook from under her bed and a purple felt-tip pen from the nightstand and began writing. She had so many ideas! So many things she wanted to find out about. So many things she wanted to do.

She wrote her name out in purple script.

Alex Mack.

She wasn't brilliant or gorgeous. She didn't sing like a bird or hit home runs when she played softball. She wasn't a carbon copy of her wonderful, perfect—well, almost perfect!—sister, Annie.

But I'm me, Alex Mack, she thought. *And maybe I can be special, too.* Maybe it was okay that she didn't know for sure yet who she was or who she was going to be.

Maybe she'd get together with Scott one day. Or maybe it would be somebody else. Someone she hadn't even met yet. Or someone in her own backyard.

Maybe she had some secret talent or interest that she just hadn't had a chance yet to discover. Alex realized it was important to keep trying new things so she wouldn't miss it, whatever it was.

Life was kind of like a mystery book. You had no

idea what was going to happen next. But Alex couldn't wait to turn the page.

The secret life of Alex Mack was still unfolding.

Maybe that was a lot more fun than already knowing all the answers, like Annie.

Who said junior high was the pits?

It might just turn out to be pretty cool after all.

About the Author

Cathy East Dubowski knows what it's like to be daughter number two, just like Alex Mack. She well remembers the day her eighth-grade algebra teacher admonished, "Don't you want to go to college like your older sister?" when she got caught writing poetry in class. In spite of her math allergy, she thinks it would be fun to relive eighth grade—especially if she could morph and zap like Alex and have a best friend like Ray. Writing *Cleanup Catastrophe!* was the next-best thing.

Cathy has written more than thirty-five books for children, including several in the Full House series published by Minstrel Books. Her book for younger readers, *Cave Boy*, was named an International Reading Association Children's Choice. Cathy never litters and practices faithful curbside recycling in North Carolina, where she lives with her husband, Mark Dubowski, a cartoonist and children's book illustrator, her very special daughters, Lauren and Megan, and their big red golden retriever, MacDougal.